THE FROGMAN AND THE SPY

Irene Preston & Liv Rancourt

THE FROGMAN AND THE SPY

ROYAL POWERS II BOOK 2

IRENE PRESTON
LIV RANCOURT

The Frogman and the Spy
© 2021 by Sharon Stoker Laurent and Amy Dunn Caldwell
www.prescourtbooks.com

ABOUT

ROYAL
POWERS

*The world of Royal Powers is not so
different from our own.
Except for the two mythical countries on
the France/Spain border.
And the two extra royal families.
Oh, and that superpowers thing.
But otherwise, you know, pretty much the
same.*

Irene Preston & Liv Rancourt

CHAPTER ONE

Jim didn't hate being a frogman, but on those rare occasions when he took time off from work, he never chose his destination with scuba diving in mind.

"Come on, Jimbo. Let's get a move on." Lori grinned at him, then shoved her mask in place. Lori, his sister, his partner, the ongoing thorn in his side. Without answering, he secured his own mask and regulator and gave her a thumbs up.

They'd moored their boat *Talisman* in a sheltered cove about three miles north of the stretch of beach belonging to the estate of Princess Odile D'Amaritz and her consort, the Duke de Champagne. The plan was simple: wait until dark, cover the distance underwater, and pick up supplies left by their reconnaissance team just outside the princess's property.

"Reconnaissance team" sounded important; really they were Jim and Lori's second cousins on their father's side. Their Abarran relations had been more than happy to help out a couple of CIA operatives who wanted to keep the peace.

An elbow to his side signaled Lori's impatience. He gave her another thumbs up and she rolled off the boat deck and landed in the water with a soft splash. When her light flashed, he hoisted her bag of tricks over the side. The waterproof bag had a light and a flotation device on top, and at her tug, he let go.

Then it was his turn. Taking one last inhale through his nose, he relaxed and exhaled, allowing himself to drop backward into the water.

The late June weather had warmed the surface, but he didn't need to go very deep before things got chilly. Jim gripped his flashlight, which would mostly be useful to allow him and Lori to communicate. At night, underwater visibility sucked.

They'd spent most of the afternoon studying maps, so he knew they just needed to keep the beach on their right and stay far enough out to avoid the breakers. Their real guide would be the waterproof smartwatch. GoogleMaps even worked underwater.

Lori's light grew dim. She had the patience of a very hungry barracuda, and he'd have to work to keep up with her once she really got going. He kicked off in her general direction and soon they were both cutting through the water.

Their fins were a new technology, fashioned after a dolphin's fin and allowing them to cover the three miles to their landing spot in less than half an hour. He'd barely found a rhythm when Lori's light pointed straight down.

In response, he did the same, stilling his legs and flipping off his flashlight. Lori's light went out and neither of them moved. The hum of a distant motor filtered through the moving water. He glanced up, scanning the water for the source of the sound. He and his sister drifted closer together, waiting for the boat to pass.

Their mission depended on secrecy. They'd called in some favors to craft identities and give them roles to play, but that work would be wasted if they were found out before they even made the beach.

The engine's hum grew louder and the keel came into sight. Jim reached for Lori's hand, and once he had her attention, he pointed in the direction of the boat. Without even their handheld lights, there was no way for him to see her expression, but the tension in her body gave him a message loud and clear.

It was too late for fishing boats to be headed out and too early for them to be coming back. There was no place between the cove they'd left and their destination for a boat to land. The princess's estate did have a pier but that was for the exclusive use of Her Highness's yacht and the powerboat toys belonging to an extended families' worth of adolescent royals.

Jim barely dared to breath in case the bubbles drew the attention of whoever was on that boat. Most likely it was an innocent late-night excursion. At worst, it was a pirate bringing a load of North Abarran wine someplace further south.

But according to chatter from some deep web sources, there were assassins at large, and their target was Princess Odile. Jim and Lori were going in to stop them.

Your mission, if you choose to accept it. Jim wondered for the millionth time why he kept accepting these missions. He could be perfectly happy at home in Napa, watching the grapes grow and bitching about how housing prices had gone through the roof.

And yeah, Lori would probably do just fine without him. Maybe better, even. But a promise was a promise, especially when it was made on his mother's deathbed.

They stalled for several long minutes, until the buzz of the boat's engine had completely dissipated. He flipped his light on and scanned their surroundings. Coral, dark rocks with their edges obscured by lichens and seaweed, the silver flashes of small fish flashing through his light. He flipped his hand in a circle, showing Lori he was ready, and when she answered, they started off again.

He dove deeper despite the cold, hoping to avoid any other random boat traffic. Lori matched his pace, and soon they were steaming full speed ahead. Glancing at his smartwatch, he made a show of pointing his light in the direction of the beach, the agreed-upon cue that they were close. Edging to the right, he followed the line on his smartwatch, letting Google take them to their target.

The water began to move, to swell and abate. Waves. Their research hadn't noted any riptides in this area, but still Jim tuned his senses, searching for a pull that would drag him off course.

Jim allowed himself to rise toward the surface, popping his ears to equilibrate the pressure. Once they were close enough to bodysurf in, he relaxed. He caught a wave and rode it till it broke, planting his feet in the sand and standing above the roiling water. Lori landed right behind him, lugging her bag of toys. Jim spit out his regulator and wordlessly caught the bag handle closest to him to help her drag it onto the beach.

They'd been promised rocks and trees and a small cabin where clothing and ID would be waiting. Everything came as billed, the cabin several hundred feet in front of them.

After pulling off their fins, they went quickly, silently, toward the cabin. Lori pushed the door open and Jim scanned the room with his flashlight. A pair of backpacks sat on an old cot, the only things not covered with a layer of dust. Jim checked the tags and picked up the one with his name on it. Waving to Lori so she'd stay put, he went back outside. The manuals didn't mention this but wearing anything under a wetsuit usually gave him an embarrassing rash, so he'd skipped the bottom layer.

And stripping naked in front of any woman, especially his sister, was a hard no.

He found a pile of rocks some twenty feet from the cottage and set the backpack on it. He pulled out a pair of shorts and a tee, then propped his flashlight so he could keep an eye on things while he changed.

Removing scuba gear was harder than putting it on, complicated by the fact that everything was wet. He shrugged out of his tank and pulled off his mask. Peeling off the wetsuit took all of his concentration, so he didn't notice the sound of someone approaching.

Which is how the stranger busted him in a full-body stretch, his personal expression of relief at having survived the water.

His one, rather major, lapse.

"Uh, hello?"

Jim blinked into the flashlight, both hands dropping to cover his junk. "Excuse me. Yeah. Hi."

The flashlight's glare prevented him from seeing who'd busted them, and for a heartbeat, Jim struggled with what to say.

"Hey Jim, did you...?" Lori came through the cabin door, fully dressed and smiling. "Oh hi! Are we on your property? I'm so sorry. We got a little off-course." She laughed, as if being caught in his birthday suit would go down in Jim's list of favorite memories.

"Go on in and change." She poked Jim in the arm, and he took the opening. He scooped up the clothing and backpack and ducked into the cabin.

Lori laughed again. "My brother and I dared each other to make a night dive, and, well, we were supposed to get back to Lesrochers but I guess we're a bit lost."

"You're about five miles north of there."

Jim parsed those few words. Mostly he heard confusion with maybe a thread of suspicion. On their own, neither he nor Lori had the kind of superpowers possessed by royalty in Abarra, but she could shoot the eye of a hummingbird from a hundred feet and he had an extraordinary sensitivity to the unspoken. If someone lied, Jim could tell as easy as breathing. And honestly, shooting a hummingbird was a neat trick, but hearing what lay behind someone's spoken words had saved them almost as many times.

He left the tee shirt untucked because the shorts were a shade tight and there wasn't a towel, so the fabric stuck to his skin. Zipping up the backpack, he headed back outside, his own flashlight aimed at their visitor.

"I'm Lori Calhoun and this is my brother Jim." Lori extended her hand in the direction of the flashlight, pushing forward so the man would either raise it or hit her in the chest.

Fortunately, he raised it, giving Jim a glance at possibly the handsomest man he'd ever seen. His mouth suddenly dry, Jim offered his own hand. "I'm Jim. Jim Calhoun."

The man regarded them both without smiling, the flashlight giving his sculped cheekbones and strong nose a dramatic cast. He shook both their hands, and although he didn't speak, Jim could feel the reluctance pouring off him in waves.

"I'm Enzo da Silva, and I'm the head groundskeeper."

"Oh wow!" Lori's laugh made Jim clench his fists to keep from slapping her. "He's your new boss, Jimbo."

Jim plastered on a smile, doing his best to look like a harmless Jimbo and not like what he was...

A spy from the United States, here in North Abarra to protect their princess before a team of assassins caused an international incident.

CHAPTER TWO

The elephants weren't cooperating.

Enzo tossed his secateurs aside and pulled the snips out of their holster at his belt. The mother and baby elephant were a tribute to Princess Katalin for her work bringing poachers in Tanzania to justice. Katalin would be arriving with her brother, the Duke of Roses, for Princess Odile's birthday. He supposed honoring a South Abarran princess in the garden of a North Abarran princess might be radical, but Enzo was a great admirer of her work. Anyway, since her brother was married to Odile's nephew, Katalin was now Odile's niece of a sort. Anything less than perfection would be an insult to both princesses.

He cast an eye toward the sun, already low enough to cast deep shadows into the hedge maze. He should wait for better light. He ran through the next day's schedule in his head and grimaced in annoyance.

They were days away from the solstice, which also happened to be Princess Odile's birthday. The combination provided an excuse for one of the largest celebrations in North Abarra. With only a few days before guests began arriving, time to linger over details in the maze was scarce.

His phone vibrated, and he pulled it out to see a text from his mother, her timing uncanny as always. *Don't forget to schedule some fun time for yourself.*

Did the elephants count as *fun time* for himself? Or was this still work? Sometimes he had trouble separating the two.

He ran a critical eye over the place where the two trunks joined. He could see the curve he wanted in his mind, but today his hands felt awkward and unsure on the snips.

The shadows were creeping closer. He needed to hurry. He gripped the snips more firmly, and placed them to make the first cut.

First be still.

Master Inigo's voice chided in his mind.

The memory calmed him. He closed his eyes, took a deep breath, then another. When he opened them, a new shadow had fallen over him, leaving his hand in darkness.

With a sigh, he removed the snips.

"You're the artist?" The Abarran was heavily accented, but the admiration was unmistakable. "Enzo, I had no idea. The sculptures are incredible."

Be still, Enzo reminded himself, before straightening on the ladder and turning to face the man casting the shadow. He didn't feel *still* when Calhoun was around. He felt restless and itchy and hungry for things he couldn't name. Or could name but shouldn't want.

He watched as the other man walked around the two elephants, as if he wanted to see every detail. He wore the same black khaki chinos and D'Amaritz Estate polo shirt as the other grounds staff, but somehow managed to look as if he'd had the uniform tailored just for him. Or maybe it just seemed that way because Enzo wasn't really seeing the clothes. Whenever he saw Jim, he remembered him the way he'd first met him, buck naked and dripping wet, like Poseidon just out of the sea. The beam of the flashlight had glinted off the rivulets of water dripping down the strong curve of his neck, over the muscles of his chest, down a taut belly to the vee of his groin where...

Enzo climbed down off the ladder, cutting off both his view of Jim and the memory.

"Jimbo," he used the brash American name his sister called him deliberately. "It's late. You're off the clock. Weren't you going into town with the rest of the crew tonight?"

Jim finished his inspection of the elephant and bent to pick up the discarded secateurs before approaching. "It's late," he agreed. "And Friday. Aren't you coming into town? Teo said you come on Fridays."

Yes, when it was just a handful of the year-round staff. Not in June when the staff included every available person they could cull from miles around and even some imported from Dulibre. Or America, as the case may be. Foreigners were actually rare. Work permits were hard to come by and usually only issued to individuals who were of Abarran descent.

Enzo wondered how Jim and Lori had managed theirs.

He realized Jim was still waiting for an answer and dredged up a smile. "Not tonight. You go on, though. I can finish clearing up the clippings here."

He expected that to be the end of it. Jim was outgoing. He had already made a lot of friends, both among the permanent staff and the army of temps. Not that Enzo had been watching. It was his job to notice how his staff was working as a team. Not just Jim.

Although at the moment he couldn't say for sure how most of the other temps were settling in.

Jim tossed the secateurs on top of the cart of clippings sitting at the "doorway" to this corner of the maze. Belatedly, Enzo noticed most of the clippings had already gone into the cart. How long had Jim been here? "You go on," he reiterated. "I can take the clippings to the compost and store the cart."

"We can walk together. It's starting to get dark. I'm not sure I can find my way out on my own." He gave Enzo a smile that said he knew exactly how to find his way out of the maze. Then he tacked on a wicked, "You wouldn't want me to wind up lost in the dark again, would you?"

Enzo almost swallowed his tongue. Did Jim *know* he had been picturing him naked? To hide his reaction, he turned to the ladder and made a production of folding it up and tucking it under his arm. Then he walked into the maze leaving Jim to follow behind, since he supposedly couldn't find his way out.

Despite himself, he smiled a little. Jim was too charming. And smart. And hot. Way too hot.

Danger. Available, possibly. But was Enzo? He examined the idea, trying to decide how risky it was. According to his heartrate and other physical indicators, the benefits would be well worth the risks. But years of training meant he wasn't at the mercy of his impulses.

He pictured the calm, smooth surface of the koi pond in the west garden, but the water rippled and churned until it became the sea instead. Waves lapped at the shore until the water parted and...*stacked stones in the sand...no water*. Water had lost its serenity for the foreseeable future.

"Did you do all the sculptures?" Jim's voice floated up from behind him.

"A lot have been here since my predecessor." This was an easy subject. "Master Inigo did them as well as designing the west garden where the koi pond is. Most of his were geometric shapes, though. The animals and other fanciful ones are mine."

Fanciful was a nice way of saying *silly*, but Enzo allowed himself the vanity this time. "The hedge maze was his creation, but he encouraged me to experiment here." The children who visited loved it anyway. "I've maintained the core structure he designed."

"The elephants are for the party, right? Because Princess Katalin will be visiting from South Abarra?"

Now how did an American know that? Enzo supposed the princess's work with animals was well documented, so maybe it wasn't so strange. He hadn't thought the American press followed her as closely as the Abarran paparazzi, though. Maybe Jim was a royal-watcher. If that were true, he would have to keep a close eye on him when the guests started arriving.

"I heard Teo talking about how the estate had ordered special moss so some new pieces would be done in time," Jim continued.

Enzo breathed a little sigh of relief. Temp workers went through a security screen, but obsessed fans were harder to weed out. He didn't want to think the only reason Jim and Lori were here was to catch an up-close glimpse of Abarran royals. Although he wasn't sure why the idea bothered him. Lots of the Abarran temps hired on for that very reason.

"Master Inigo would have never used moss," he answered. "But I didn't have an existing hedge that could have been shaped into something this unique and even if I had, it would have taken too long. The moss allows me to," *play*, he almost said. "Produce more quickly for special events and I don't have to worry as much about making mistakes." Except with the elephants. There was no time to grow out any ill-advised cuts if he screwed up now.

"But Teo said it took months." They had reached the exit of the maze and Jim pushed the cart a little faster until they were walking side by side. He had picked the side without the ladder between them and they were almost shoulder to shoulder. "How do you find time? When they told me I'd be reporting to the groundskeeper, I thought they meant whoever was in charge of the formal areas. But Teo said you manage everything, the gardens, the forest, hay production, the orchard and..." he hesitated, "some kind of environmental research the Abarran government is funding here and in the National Forrest?"

"Land management for CO2 mitigation," Enzo murmured. *Teo* had told him that? His research wasn't a thing they talked about even though Teo did help him with a lot of the actual execution. "I'm part of an international research consortium. Really, I just collect data and add it to the group database for analysis."

"So you must work with people from all over the world." Jim sounded admiring, as though Enzo were some kind of sophisticate, jetting off all over the world to confer with his colleagues. Globe-trotting for causes was his mother's thing. Enzo was happier staying on the estate. Except maybe during solstice week when his research took an extreme backseat to birthday festivities.

"The internet is an international community, especially for scientists." He couldn't bring himself to completely destroy Jim's flattering viewpoint. He supposed he did know people from all over the world. He had never thought of it like that.

They had reached the service area on the far side of the estate. He helped Jim unload the clippings from the cart into the industrial composter, then store the cart in one of the outbuildings. Despite the fact that Jim was a virtual stranger, the work felt companionable, their rhythm almost as in sync as when he worked with Teo, whom Enzo had known since grade school. Except Teo was a friend and companion. He didn't have this constant sense of Teo as a man. Teo's scent didn't tease him as they stood next to each other outside the utility barn. He didn't have to work to stop picturing Teo naked.

"The crew will be at Le Bouleau. You can still catch them up."

Jim raised an eyebrow. "We could. I'll buy you a glass of wine. You could tell me more about your work."

Tempting. Enzo bit back the automatic *yes* that tried to escape. No one on the estate asked about his work except his mother, who was rarely here, and Princess Odile, who wanted a tab in his monthly report. And having a glass of wine with a handsome companion had its own appeal.

The invitation in Jim's eyes as he waited for an answer held a stronger allure than the wine, but Enzo had a schedule and a daily checklist. He had completed neither yet. In the end, duty won. Knowing he had met his own standards was more rewarding in the long run than the temporary pleasure of the outing.

Le Bouleau would be noisy and crowded with strangers. An extrovert like Jim would find plenty of companionship.

He made his voice friendly but firm as he reestablished boundaries. "Not tonight. But enjoy yourself. Thanks for staying late to help out. You can flex some of your hours next week or log the overtime, whichever you prefer."

He didn't wait for a response as he turned and headed through the woods toward his own cottage. But he turned back at the sound of his name.

"Hey, da Silva." Jim stood with his arms outstretched, palms up. "Are you always this stubborn?"

"Pardon me?"

Jim grinned, looking cocky and way too appealing. "I don't give up, you know. In fact, some might say that I'm pretty much unstoppable."

Enzo cocked his head, not sure where this was going. "So?"

"Well, you know what happens when an unstoppable force meets an immovable object, don't you?"

"No."

Jim winked. "I can't be giving it away. You'll just have to wait and see."

This time it was Jim who turned and walked away. Enzo stared after him, amused and tempted. Then he resolutely headed home.

CHAPTER THREE

The next morning at 0700 sharp, the entire crew met outside the greenhouse for Enzo to give them their assignments for the day, and after two weeks, Jim had the routine down.

Standing in the back row where his height wouldn't block others' view, Jim slapped on a cockeyed smile and waited to hear how he'd spend the day. He and two other men had been constructing a temporary amphitheater where bands would play and since he fully expected he'd draw another amphitheater card, he let his gaze wander over the crowd.

Enzo stood in front of them, his dark, fearsome features and loose linen clothing better suited to a fashion spread than to ticking things off on an iPad as he assigned people to tasks.

"Rollie, you and Bennet prune around the folly," Enzo said. "Marshall and Frank have the amphitheater, and"—he raised his gaze from the tablet, glanced at Jim, then immediately went back to the iPad—"Calhoun and Herve, you two start in the stables. The princess is going to ride before lunch, and I want it so clean she can eat off the floor if she wants to."

Jim's goofball smile didn't slip, though he was busy calculating this unexpected turn. He hadn't eliminated any possible suspects, yet, but something about Herve pinged his spydar. Working alongside the landscaper was an opportunity to catch a lie at the source, though what Jim knew about horses could fit in a matchbox.

Lori was going to laugh her ass off when she heard this one.

Once everyone had a task for the morning, they were dismissed. Jim accidentally-on-purpose caught Enzo's gaze again, however, before he could come up with an excuse to say something, Herve brushed past him.

Business before pleasure, now.

With that in mind, Jim pivoted and followed him, pulling up all he'd learned about the man since their arrival. Herve had a traveling companion named Armand. The two held themselves apart from the rest of the crew, though Jim couldn't tell if they had suspicious motivations or were just antisocial.

The stable was the final destination of the mile-long cobblestone drive that came from the two-lane highway to the estate. Jim did know how to ride, and he figured he could push a broom and lift a shovel with the best of them, but he surely hoped Herve would know where the things he shoveled and swept should go, and in what order. They'd sat at the same table in a pub one night, and since Jim listened more than he talked, he'd learned that Herve had a girlfriend in Catalina. At least he had an ice-breaker if he needed one.

They approached the stable slowly, and darned if it didn't seem like that building grew larger the closer they got. They stopped in front of it, Herve with his arms crossed, Jim with his fists on his hips.

"You ever mucked out a stable before?" he asked, and for a moment, he thought Herve wouldn't answer. He just stood there with his arms crossed, his jaw getting tighter and tighter.

"I'm sure that's all the princess thinks I'm good for."

Jim blinked at the bitterness in the other man's voice and for a second, his *aw shucks* grin faltered. "I'm not sure what you mean."

Herve glared at him, one strong finger pointed at his own chin. "Look at me. You can't tell I'm Romani? She thinks I got horses in my blood, and Enzo humors her. I could hack into her laptop faster than I can clean a stall, but he sticks me in the stable like a decoration." He broke off, pausing a moment as if waiting for Jim's reaction. "Come on. Let's get this done."

Jim decided that now was definitely not the time to describe his limited experience, so he followed Herve in through the huge double doors and grabbed the first shovel he saw. He was on his way to the closest stall when Herve stopped him.

"Hey, asshole. What are you doing?"

Jim turned slowly, not sure he should let the insult slide. "I'm going to clean out a stall."

Herve snorted. "Not that one, unless you want to die."

Glancing at the stall in question, Jim tried to figure out where he'd gone wrong. The stall's occupant stood taller than the stall door. The horse possessed a long, graceful neck, a deep chocolate coat, and delicate features.

The horse was also flaring its nostrils and giving the occasional impatient stamp with a hoof.

"Do we take them out of the stall before we clean it?"

Herve scratched his head. "You're joking, right?" He shook his head at Jim's raised eyebrow. "Just shove the horse to the side and get to work. If they won't stay out of the way, send them into the pasture and don't let them back in until you're done."

His scowl would have made a lesser man blanch. Jim just tried not to roll his eyes.

"Here." Herve pointed into the back of the barn. "Go down there where there are some empty stalls. I'll deal with Neutron."

"Neutron, like the bomb?"

The horse in question nickered, as if laughing at Jim's joke.

"Neutron, like the stallion who throws anyone except the Duke de Champagne. Best you don't go anywhere near him."

Giving him a two-finger salute, Jim headed down the hall in the center of the barn. He rarely got tired of playing an easy-going character, but Herve's attitude stuck in his craw.

Maybe because you recognize trouble after seeing it so often in your own damned mirror.

With a snort, Jim set aside the negative attitude he had no time to indulge. He passed between a row of stables on his right, maybe twenty in all. On his left was a tack room, offices, and a large space filled with bales of hay.

And a conveniently placed barrel of apples. *Sweet.*

The farthest stalls were empty. Jim gave each a quick inspection, but no random visitors had left deposits on the worn plank floor. The first occupied stall housed a sleepy-looking donkey. Jim banged on the stall door to draw the donkey's attention. The look he got could have been in Webster's Dictionary under baleful. *Could donkeys even look baleful? Why didn't the damned CIA give me a class in animal husbandry?*

Jim did note the gate at the rear of the stall, leading to the run Herve had mentioned. "Here goes nothing." He opened the door to the donkey's stall and stepped inside. The donkey watched, his expression shifting from baleful to bored. Closing the door, Jim went in further, aiming to slide past the beast on his way to the gate.

The beast, er, donkey, apparently had other ideas. It shifted in his direction, effectively pinning Jim against the wall of the stall. It managed to avoid stepping directly on his foot, and the amount of pressure wasn't painful at all, but still.

"Er, donkey? Mr. Donkey? Would you like a treat?" Maybe Jim should have started with the bribe. At any rate, he held the apple near the donkey's nose.

The donkey shifted again, this time in the opposite direction. Jim brought his hand closer, and in seconds the donkey chomped.

That was his cue.

While the donkey chewed happily on the apple, Jim opened the gate. The beast must have recognized the noise because it backed out, still chewing. When Jim had the stall to himself, he went to work. He dragged one of the wagons over and filled it with soiled straw and donkey pooh.

He happened to notice Herve dragging a loaded wagon to the front of the barn, which gave him his next step. Following Herve's cue, he found the discard pile, emptied his wagon, and rolled to a pile of fresh hay adjacent to the front door. He slowed down so he had time to observe how Herve used the clean hay to make a new bed for Neutron.

Huh. Should have watched how he convinced the stallion to go out in its run without getting stepped on.

They worked stall by stall until they met in the middle. By then Herve had apparently decided he was the one in charge, and he set Jim to sweeping while he went off and did...other things? Jim wasn't sure where the hell Herve went, but he didn't have time to worry. Enzo had said he wanted the place clean enough for a princess and they weren't there yet.

He'd finished sweeping the main walkway down the center of the barn when Lori poked her head in the door. "Princess incoming," she stage-whispered, and sure enough, the barn's double doors opened and a small group of people entered.

There was Lori, dressed in a uniform similar to the one worn by the grounds crew, and an older woman in the same togs. Lori carried a clipboard and pen, while the older woman had a tablet with a small stylet.

Enzo da Silva was with them, too. He'd replaced his loose linen shirt with a black crewneck that gave Jim way too much information about the cut of his pecs and the bulge of his biceps. There were two other men dressed similarly to Enzo, identifying them as staff rather than guests.

Neutron the stallion must have been attracted by their arrival because he came to the door of his stall.

"Is that who I'll ride?"

The question was posed by a woman of a certain age, with the thick straight hair and strong features common to the wealthy. She took a few steps closer to Neutron's stall.

"No Poppy dear, that's Bob's horse." In those few words, a dark-haired woman with long nails and tasteful highlights made it plain she was the princess, *thank you very much.* "We'll take Guinevere and Methuselah. Groom?"

Jim glanced up from the tack room door to see the whole group looking in his direction. The princess, the reason for their involvement, waved him over.

"Could you please bring our horses around?"

Before Jim responded, they heard a sharp pop, as if someone had stepped on a piece of bubble wrap. Everyone jumped, but Neutron, well, Neutron took the noise personally. He reared up on his hind legs, kicking the door of his stall open. He was all white eyes and flared nostrils and flashing hooves, and Poppy dear stood frozen right in front of him.

Jim didn't know what the hell to do for the horse, but since everyone else was stuck like a flock of deer in the headlights, he darted around the little group and scooped Poppy dear up, carrying her out of the range.

Neutron brought his hooves down hard, shocking people into action. Enzo reached for the princess and Lori got her older coworker clear. The two men dressed in company colors went for the horse. One got a hand on his halter, keeping the horse from rearing again, and in a surprisingly short amount of time, they had him under control.

Meanwhile, Jim set Poppy on the ground. She stared up at him, blue eyes shining. "You saved my life."

For once, Lori didn't laugh at him. She bustled the VIPs outside and, when Herve appeared from wherever he'd hidden, she instructed him to start saddling horses.

Jim offered to help, but Herve scoffed at him so Jim left him to it. Instead, he made a circuit of the barn, looking for where Herve might have been working, and what could have set Neutron off, and wondering whether those two things were connected.

CHAPTER FOUR

The near-miss with Neutron wouldn't stop playing in his head.

Enzo crossed his left leg over his left arm, tucked his toes under his right arm, and shifted forward into omkarasana. His body settled into the pose and he focused on his breath. Only his breath, not the sight of Jim plucking Poppy, Marchioness Rousse, literally from under Neutron's hooves.

A near disaster wasn't a disaster and it was only the first of many that were sure to occur over the next two weeks. Everything was under control.

He breathed out on the reminder.

Eleven months out of the year, Enzo's life on D'Aramitz Estate was idyllic. Most of the princess's visitors were family and required little extra effort.

He had plenty of staff. His estate duties were routine leaving plenty of time for his research.

But during June everything that could go wrong usually did. You couldn't swell the population of the estate and local village by tenfold and not expect chaos.

The word *chaos* brought Jim to mind again, the sight of Neutron's hooves millimeters from his head.

The balance to chaos was order. Calm.

Enzo breathed into his diaphragm, annoyed to realized sweat had collected on his brow despite the cool pre-dawn air. He blinked away a drop that rolled into his eyes. *Be still.* He pictured a smooth stone, tracing the pattern of striations with his mind's eye. *Breathe.*

Behind him a twig snapped.

Plop.

The imaginary stone fell into a pool of water, sending ripples eddying out from the impact.

"Heya, that looks uncomfortable."

Enzo took a deep breath, blinked away the mental image of the stone sinking into the water, and released himself from the pose. Released. Not fell out of. He answered without turning around.

"Good morning, Jim."

"Nice place you got here. Hope I didn't disturb you. It seems I'm turned around again."

He heard more footsteps at the edge of the terrace and a second later Jim appeared in his field of vision. He had dressed for running in a sleeveless athletic top, shorts, and running shoes. Sweat gleamed on every inch of his skin.

Enzo's mouth went dry. He was proud of the fact that his breathing stayed steady. The increase in his heartrate was almost imperceptible. He rolled to his feet.

"I was almost done," he said, sidestepping the question. Jim disturbed him on multiple levels, but there was no sense in telling him so.

"I see you like to get an early start, too." Jim smiled, as though this were a bonding experience. "'Course I'm not much for the yoga. Give me a nice long run in the morning to clear the cobwebs out. There's something empowering about being up and about before everyone else, isn't there? Kinda feels like the whole world is there just for you."

"How American."

Jim shrugged good naturedly, his eyes still on Enzo. "Maybe I should rethink the yoga. More flexibility is always attractive."

The word attractive held a subtle emphasis. Enzo was suddenly aware he was wearing nothing but a pair of yoga leggings. Jim wasn't ogling him, but he still looked pretty flushed. Perhaps more so than the run accounted for.

"Would you like some juice?" Maybe he wasn't the only one thirsty. Enzo turned the idea over in his head as he opened the door and gestured for Jim to proceed him.

"That would sure hit the spot if you have extra."

"Of course."

Enzo led the most dangerous man he had met in years into his kitchen and watched him drink a glass of mango puree.

"I should have known you aren't a coffee person." Jim licked a drop of the juice off his top lip. "This is delicious. What's the brand? I'll have to get some for myself."

"It's local fruit. I puree it myself."

"I should have guessed."

"Oh?"

"Eating local is 'green,' right? Makes sense. You do all the environmental research, solar panels on the roof, and isn't your mother a spokesperson for some eco-group?"

Enzo raised an eyebrow. "Zha Zsi? You are a gossip, aren't you? But you're right, she installed the solar panels years ago."

"This is her house? I didn't get the impression she lived in the area."

"Her work keeps her on the road most of the year. The house has been in the family for generations."

"It's not part of the royal estate?"

"Sometime in the past, maybe. What about you? Where are you from?" Enzo gently redirected the conversation. Not that he wasn't proud of his mother, but discussion of the organizations she worked for could get uncomfortable as could explanations of their exact relationship with the royal family.

Jim affably moved on to other topics, until they both noticed the time. June meant no weekends off. But when he offered to point Jim in the direction of the staff quarters, the other man looked surprised.

"Won't you be going that way?"

"After I shower."

"I'll wait. Wouldn't want to get lost again and be late."

Enzo threw him a sharp look, wondering if Jim was really directionally challenged or if this was just another demonstration of *unstoppable force*.

There was no polite way to call him on it though, so Enzo nodded, then went upstairs to shower and try not to think of moonlit water.

Enzo purposely assigned Jim to the crew setting up a camping area for the younger royals about a mile from the main house. The camping had been Teo's idea a few years back when it became obvious that the princess's birthday bash had exceeded critical mass in terms of available lodging either on the estate itself or in the surrounding towns. It was a clever solution that solved both the lack of bed space and the kids' desire to escape near constant adult supervision at an officially-unofficial State event. Not that anyone left a few dozen young supos completely to their own devices, but the campsite was safely within the borders of the estate and security was discreet.

This year, the campsite also solved, at least for a day, the problem of what to do with Jim, who seemed determined to keep intruding on Enzo's personal space.

Unfortunately, out of sight did not mean out of mind.

By mid-afternoon with Jim nowhere in sight, Enzo was hot, bothered, and sick of trying to visualize stones.

A stone resists the force of the river. Master Inigo's words came to him. *But in the end, the stone is worn away and the river still flows. Be the river, not the stone.*

Maybe he was making this more complicated than it was. Maybe he should go with the flow on this one. Jim had made it more than obvious the attraction cut both ways.

The more he turned the idea over in his head, the more reasonable it seemed.

"Enzo? *Yoo hooo.* Mr. da Silva?"

"Over here, Lori." Enzo detoured out of the hedge. The elephants would have to wait. Again.

It seemed both the Calhouns had a talent for invading his space.

Lori popped around the corner of the maze with a bright smile on her face. Enzo forced himself to smile back. Jim's sister had his eyes and wide mouth, but she hadn't relied on the sun to lighten her hair. The combination of white-blonde hair and brown eyes elevated her appearance from pretty to compelling. Next to Jim's height, Lori was an unassuming five foot five, but what she lacked in height she made up for in personality.

If Jim was charismatic, Lori was impossibly perky. She had been hired on as an extra housekeeper but somehow caught the princess's eye. When the regular event planner fell ill, Lori had perked her way into a giant promotion. She was now the event liaison between the princess and the planner, who was theoretically still running things from her hospital bed. Enzo had his doubts about who was in charge.

Lori seemed to be everywhere at once and the staff had started calling her Lori Le Lapin after the

Energizer Bunny. Frankly, she scared the shit out of him.

Coming out of the maze to find her casually tossing a large hammer into the air and catching it did nothing to calm his nerves.

"I know it's not your job," she gave him a brilliant smile, as if that were going to make whatever came next okay, "but we're short-staffed inside and I need a big ol' man to help us hang a picture. You don't mind, do you?"

He did, actually. But he doubted declining the request was an option. Instead he followed her, ready to hold whatever it was she wanted held long enough to pound a nail in.

He realized with dismay they weren't heading for one of the family rooms, but the grand gallery. He could hear the princess before he saw her. "No, no. Not that one. The *ugly* one. To the left. Your *other* left."

Lori barreled through the door ahead of him. "I brought reinforcements, ma'am. We'll get this done, don't worry."

"Enzo." The princess beamed at him. "Just look what my nephew the Duke of Arles sent for my birthday. It's a portrait of Smookie by Remy Marchand. Oh, that naughty boy. Tarik told me Remy was booked out a year at least and the whole time he was planning this."

Sure enough, a giant portrait of the princess's fat pug, Smookie, was propped against the wall. The artist, best-known for his stunning landscapes and impressions of everyday people, was highly in demand and could pick and choose his commissions. Enzo figured Tarik had talked him into painting

Smookie by offering to pay by the inch. Undoubtedly, the artist had captured Smookie's wrinkled face, slightly protruding eyes, and floppy ears to perfection, but Enzo found an eight-foot tall Smookie head more than a little creepy.

The princess obviously didn't share his view. She focused her attention back on the gallery wall. A cantilever ladder had been rolled into the room. The platform had been raised to around sixteen feet. Teo stood at the base and Herve stood atop the platform gesturing at the wall.

"Left, left," shouted the princess.

Teo pushed the ladder left until Herve was in front of the largest painting in the room, a group of shepherdesses frolicking with their flock on a pastoral hillside.

"That's the one," the princess called. "Get that ridiculous thing down. They can go straight to the attic and we'll put Smookie up."

Enzo eyed the painting uneasily. He didn't know much about art, but he was pretty sure the shepherdesses were by Jean-Honoré Fragonard and belonged in a museum. Of more immediate concern, the painting was even larger than Smookie and displayed in an ornate gold frame. Herve leaned over the safety rail.

"Just a minute, Herve," Enzo cautioned. He turned to the princess. "Ma'am, I believe it might be best if..."

"Go on, Herve," the princess countermanded. "Tarik will be here for my birthday and I want him to see how much I love his gift. Down with the shepherdesses!"

Herve leaned out again and grasped the top of the frame. "Little closer, Teo."

"Wait, and I'll help," Enzo yelled. They should at least lock the wheels on the ladder. And Herve was an ox of a man, but the painting was bulky and had to weigh a ton in that huge frame.

It was too late. As soon as Teo nudged the ladder forward Herve grunted and lifted the painting up and free of its moorings. For a second, Enzo thought he had been wrong, that Herve would be able to wrestle the painting onto the platform where they could eventually get it down.

But no one had actually thought that far ahead. The safety rail was between the bottom half of the painting and the platform. No matter how Herve grunted, he couldn't lift the huge frame high enough to get it over the rail and onto the platform. "Teo, come up and help me," he ordered.

Teo started up the steps.

The princess darted forward, to just under the platform, shouting up encouragements.

"Ma'am." Enzo rushed toward her. "Stay back, ma'am."

As Herve continued to wrestle with the painting, the ladder, no longer steadied by Teo, rolled slightly to the left.

Lori seemed to see the danger, too. She left off whatever she was doing to the painting of Smookie and made a beeline for the ladder. Unfortunately, her beeline for the ladder intersected with Enzo's beeline for the princess. Enzo found himself on the floor without quite understanding what had happened.

Everyone seemed to be shouting. Lori was cursing furiously. The princess continued yelling at Herve and Teo. Herve barked out a series of contradictory instructions to Teo. Teo kept repeating, "I've almost got it. I've almost got it," as though saying it made it true.

Down the hall, Enzo heard yet another voice, a familiar male voice, calling Lori's name.

Before he could wonder what Jim was doing back from the campsite, his attention was caught by Teo's triumphant shout, "I've *got* it." And then, "No, don't let..."

There was a mighty crash as the painting swung sideways and down. Herve and Teo leaned over the rail, hands desperately clutching the gilded frame as the painting rocked back and forth hitting both the wall and the ladder. The momentum of the impact jolted the ladder away from the wall and it began to roll faster, directly toward the princess with the picture swinging wildly overhead. Rather than run, the princess spread her arms. "I'll catch it!"

Enzo made a desperate attempt to get to his feet, but he and Lori seemed inexplicably entwined. He hit the floor a second time just as he heard Teo's panicked, *"I'm losing it."*

CHAPTER FIVE

He lost it.

Damn.

Jim had one of those *time turns to crystal* moments. The ladder spun like a slow-mo amusement park ride. Herve's mouth made a near-perfect *Oh* of shock. Lori and Enzo lay tangled in a squirming heap. And the princess — whom he'd last seen when he yanked her friend out from under a horse — stood on tiptoe, arms raised like a chalice of hope.

Because hope was all she had going for her. Unless her superpower involved floating 250- pound artwork above the ground, she was going to get hurt.

Jim amended the phrase to "We're both gonna get hurt" and ran like hell in her direction. He had a good six or eight inches on her ladyship but his angle was wrong. At best he'd be able to deflect the painting and send it to the floor and with a little luck, the shattering glass wouldn't gouge too big a hole in the canvas.

He managed to get a hand on the corner of the frame without bowling the princess over like she was the center of ten pins. He gripped it hard, but the frame wrenched out of his grasp.

Wrenched free and floated about six feet off the ground, the air around it swirling.

The glow from Princess Odile's smile could have been seen from the moon. "It worked!" She lowered her arms and the painting drifted gently to the floor. Brushing her hands together, she grinned at them. "Not bad for an old girl."

Jim scrambled mentally through his background notes. The princess was a registered supo and her power had something to do with the wind. "You made a mini tornado?"

She couldn't have looked more pleased. "I certainly did. I'm a little out of practice or I would have come up with something more showy."

Lori bounded over. "That was fantastic!"

Enzo hurried behind her, his baggy pants fluttering. "Are you sure you're okay?"

Princess Odile gave him a squelching look. "Absolutely. Now gentlemen, get those wanton shepherdesses into the attic and hang up my Smookie, please. And you"—she jabbed a perfectly-manicured nail at Lori—"Lapin, you come with me. The caterer should be at my office in fifteen minutes."

Jim vowed he'd never let Lori forget her nickname was 'rabbit' while Herve and Teo wrestled the offending artwork off the floor.

"Did y'all need a hand with that?" Jim put on his widest smile and headed in their direction. He knew from experience that he was more effective if he added a touch of the Abbaran equivalent of a southern accent to his Ugly American schtick. It made people doubt his intelligence, which gave him an advantage.

Enzo stepped forward, still settling his ruffled feathers. "I thought I assigned you to the kids camp."

"Correct, sir." Jim didn't let his heightened amusement show. Enzo was cute when he was flustered. It put cracks in his impenetrable-zen persona. "I left the others finishing the last yurt and figured I'd come on up here for further instructions."

Herve and Teo managed to hoist the painting through the gallery door without Jim's help, which was unfortunate. Jim had hoped to hear Herve describe what had happened. Was it truly an unfortunate accident? Or had a would-be assassin taken advantage of circumstances?

Would Jim hear the lie, or simply the echo of a truth unsaid?

After the horse incident, Jim had tried to catch Herve but the erstwhile groundsman had proved to be elusive. Jim had managed to run Herve's friend Armand to ground, but the man's evasive non-answers hadn't helped.

Jim needed to hear it from the horse's mouth. *Herve, not Neutron.*

Chuckling at his own bad pun, Jim turned his attention to Enzo. The head groundsman was hoisting a large painting in the direction of the ladder.

A portrait of the world's most pampered pug. A pug that judged them and found them wanting.

"Here," Jim said. "Let me give you a hand with that."

Enzo brushed him off. "I'll wait till the others get back. If the yurts are set up, see if you can find the guys who were working with you and take them down to the boathouse. Do you know much about sailing?"

"A bit." Jim's cheeks were getting tired from holding that smug smile in place. He knew enough about boats of all kinds to have piloted a yacht from Marseille to the coast of Abarra. Well, Lori might dispute which of them had been the pilot, but the point remained. Jim could sail anything from a dinghy to a cabin cruiser.

"There are a number of sailboats and a few kayaks. Make sure everything is in order for our guests to use them."

Enzo's tone didn't leave Jim much wiggle room for debate, so he gave a two-finger salute and went out into the sunshine. *Make sure everything is in order* left a lot to his imagination. Jim might need to take one of the kayaks out to make sure it was seaworthy. And *oh, by the way*, he could make a quick trip to the *Talisman* to grab the laptop he hadn't packed for his frogman swim.

He'd been short-sighted not to anticipate the need to do a little cyber-stalking. Because while Jim wasn't inclined to suspect Enzo of having designs on the princess, he couldn't deny that the groundskeeper's mother had an interesting story, and his father was pretty much a question mark.

No, he hadn't ruled anyone out entirely.

Jim made a cursory trip to the campground, relieved to find his workmates had gone off to other adventures. He backtracked half a mile or so to the point where the path forked. One branch went back to the main house, the other led to the beach.

The stables were on his right, and an older man was saddling Neutron. The man's bearing had the unconscious arrogance of a supo, and his perfectly-groomed hair with its touch of silver at the temples spoke of wealth.

The Duke de Champagne.

Only the duke could ride Neutron, Herve had said, and apparently only the duke could make the beast behave. Neutron of the wild eyes and flashing hooves stood as placid as a cow while the duke fussed with his bridle. The duke had the power to calm animals, which could come in handy under the right circumstances.

Like when the big stallion Neutron needed to stretch his legs.

Jim picked up his pace before someone spotted him and volunteered to help him out with the boats. That was the downside to making himself everyone's best friend; they all wanted to hang out with him. Fortunately, Neutron required all of the duke's attention, and there was no one else about.

He found the boathouse quite close to the spot where he and Lori had come to shore, a couple hundred feet away from the hut where they'd changed clothes. The boathouse had been constructed of the same materials as the rest of the estate: white stucco with a red tile roof and a bougainvillea climbing the wall on the water side.

Inside he found five kayaks hung on wooden racks, each painted down the center with a distinctive blue and white stripe. The sailboats were tied up to a small dock that jutted out into the cerulean sea, their masts and booms bare. Further down the beach a stone patio surrounded a fire pit, with a row of pillars holding a mix of grape and flowering vines to make a roof.

This place is all set up for a party.

A pile of white canvas sat on the boathouse floor, a clue that Enzo's vague instructions likely included rigging the sails. A light breeze blew off the water, more than enough to power one of the sailboats, but Jim decided a kayak suited his purposes better.

He needed to be there and back again with a minimum of fuss, so he pulled a kayak off its rack and grabbed a paddle. In minutes he was powering along, just outside the breakers, following the coast. Running across the current meant staying the course took his full attention. Well, most of his attention. He had time to admire the rugged coastline and the swirl of the waves as they rolled up over the rocks.

This place spoke to him in a way the California coastline didn't, which was weird, because the Bay Area was home.

Had to be rehashed childhood memories. Right?

He paused, paddle poised over the water, and let the atmosphere — the sun, the salt, the humid heat — soak in, but only for a moment. "Come on," he muttered. "Let's get this done before you test this thing's hull against those rocks."

Paddling on, he found Talisman with no difficulty, and after lashing the kayak to the yacht, he climbed aboard.

Other than a few piles of seabird droppings and a coiled rope that something had knocked out of place, the deck looked the same as when they'd left it. The cabin had a similar air of disuse, and after a quick scan, Jim unlocked the tackle box where he'd left his laptop.

His official employer, the one he'd taken leave from when Lori had brought the threat to the princess to his attention, had a satellite server he could access from anywhere. Lori had emailed him a list of everyone who was involved in the party preparations, from the caterer and his crew to the extra housemaids to the raft of people who'd shown up to work the grounds and play waiter and waitress at the more formal events.

He started by feeding each name into an international database of known criminals. Anyone who had anything more serious than a parking ticket on their records was on this list. That action generated a shorter list, one that didn't contain the names Herve or Armand. He copied the list and set it aside.

Opening a new browser page, he logged into a powerful genealogy site, something the general public would never know about. He took his full list and entered the names, limiting the search to two generations. This brought his cache of names from around three hundred to just under twelve thousand.

"All righty then," he murmured, scanning the expanded list. Going back to the criminal database, he entered the expanded list in groups of five hundred. When he was done, he had a list of who had been naughty and whose parents or grandparents had wandered outside the limits of the law.

To his shock — and dismay — the name Enzo da Silva appeared on the second list. Enzo's maternal grandfather had been arrested at a protest in 1968 in the Basque city of San Sebastien.

Jim hummed to himself. "Seems Grandad was something of a radical."

The next entry shut him right up. Enzo's father had never been arrested, but he was a known associate of a radical anti-supo group. "Well, damn." The winner of the Most Likely to Assassinate a Princess award was the same guy who'd never once made Jim's radar ping.

That alone was enough to make him suspicious.

He narrowed the search further by eliminating certain crimes — anything traffic, domestic, or white collar-related he pulled into a separate list, leaving primarily those with violence or politics in their history.

No Herve. No Armand. Yes Enzo.

"Well smack my ass and call me Sally." Jim shook his head, saving the results of his work. He sent Lori a secure message, sharing half the list with her and asking her to do some background digging.

He made sure Enzo-and-family stayed on his own list.

Figuring he'd been missing for long enough, he shut down the laptop and stowed it in a leather satchel for the paddle back to the princess's estate. Out on deck, he stopped for a moment, breathing the sea air and coming to terms with what he was going to have to do.

He was going to stick to Enzo like a bad spray tan, so that if the guy really did have something to do with the plot, Jim would be well-placed to stop it. And if they ended up in position to act on the attraction that swirled between them, well, fog of war and all.

And if seducing a man to break the case made Jim feel slimy, he'd just have to suck it up and shower afterwards.

His thoughts were interrupted by someone hollering. The isolated cove where they'd stashed *Talisman* was surrounded on three sides by rocky ridges that rose dark and craggy out of the ocean. A man on horseback sat on the ridge across from Jim, waving in his direction. Squinting brought the proud bearing of horse and man into focus. The Duke of Champagne on Neutron.

"Hey!" Jim waved back, wondering how much trouble he was in.

"You're from my estate, or rather that kayak is."

Damn. The paint job. "Yes sir. I'm Jim Calhoun." Jim broadened his accent, bringing up Jimbo's goofball grin. "And you're the duke?"

"The Duke of Champagne, yes. Pleasure to meet you."

The duke's words held an subtle resonance, the kind Jim's extra sense used to identify a lie. "Enzo asked me to make sure the kayaks were all sea-worthy."

The duke — or whomever he was — frowned and Jim had to wonder how much product it took to hold that perfect coiffure while riding a stallion.

"And did Enzo also ask you to board random vessels?"

"Oh no, sir. This here belongs to my uncle."

The man made a show of surveying the yacht from one end to the other. "And will your...uncle...be attending the princess's birthday soiree?"

The downside of Jim's semi-power was that he could tell if someone told a lie, but he didn't know the truth. From this distance, the lie could have been "I'm the duke." It could also have been "Pleasure to meet you."

Unless the wind and water between them distorted the sound. Either way, he couldn't discount the idea that the duke had something to do with the threat against the princess.

Either way he'd best go along with it. "Yes sir, I'm pretty sure he is." Or he could be. The same family who'd prepped things for Jim and Lori lived in the area and pretty much the whole community showed up at the princess's estate at some point over the four-day event.

"You'll have to bring him to the dinner we're holding the night before things begin. I look forward to meeting him."

Though there was some distance between them, the duke's smug suspicion carried over the restless murmur of the sea.

"I'll be sure he's there," Jim said.

"Good." The duke waved, gathering the reins in his other hand.

"Thank you, sir."

The rider brought Neutron around and had soon dropped behind the rocky edge of the cliff. Jim stood for another moment, then shot Lori a quick text message.

Going to need to ask the cousins if they know someone who can play uncle.

He made a reminder for himself: figure out if the "duke" is lying.

CHAPTER SIX

As the solstice approached, the days grew longer and longer. Unfortunately, they didn't gain any extra hours. This year, the big day fell on the weekend, which meant the biggest events — private, public, and State — would be hyper-concentrated over two days instead of spread out over a full week. Even most of the family wouldn't start arriving until Wednesday.

Tuesday night, Enzo figured, was his last chance to grab a break before full madness descended upon them.

It was also the night he finally let Jim convince him to go to dinner.

To his surprise, Jim didn't suggest one of the nearby pubs. Instead, he led Enzo down to the waterfront to the pier, where a small sailboat was moored.

Enzo eyed the boat. "I thought we were having dinner."

"We'll get there. I thought this would appeal to your environmental side." He looked pleased with himself. "No motor pollution. Anyway, it's an amazing day. I couldn't resist being on the water."

He hopped onboard and Enzo followed. He had lived on the sea all his life and been invited onboard the royal yachts multiple times. His piloting experience was mostly limited to his own little hobie cat, though. At around twenty-five feet, the sloop should be manageable by one person, but they would have to know what they were doing. If Jim didn't intend to use the motor, casting off and docking would be an adventure. He surveyed the set-up, resigning himself to playing crew.

As though reading his mind, Jim laughed back at him. "Get comfortable, I got this."

Enzo spent the next few minutes watching Jim make getting underway look easy. He was surefooted and relaxed in the way only someone who spent a lot of time on the water could be. For a big guy, he was also surprisingly graceful, with an economy of movement that showed off his athleticism.

Jim had traded his estate uniform for belted white shorts, a light blue button down, and deck shoes. The shirt had been shrugged off and tossed into the little cabin within seconds of boarding. Enzo couldn't unglue his eyes from tanned back, muscled legs, and a lightly-furred chest just as sun-lightened as the hair on his head.

At 6 pm just days before the solstice, they had plenty of sunlight left. Mother Nature had provided a perfect Abarran late-spring day with sky and sea so blue they merged into a bowl at the horizon. For once, Master Inigo — *live in the moment* — and his mother — *do something for yourself* — were in agreement. Enzo left the impending birthday bash, global warming, and an urgent text from Teo about increasing security on the shore. He tilted his head back and let himself sink into the moment, the warm sun, briny sea air, and the sight of Jim, his own head angled to catch the same sun and wind.

"I could spend all day out here," Jim drawled.

"Diving?"

"Nah." His voice was dreamy. "Just this. I could spend my whole life like this."

Enzo couldn't think of a response. The idea of a whole day, much less a whole life, spent drifting on the sea wouldn't process.

The incomprehensible idea lodged in the back of his mind like a burr snagged into the fabric of his own life. He tried to think of something he did that inspired a similar sentiment. His time in the forest came closest, although that had more purpose. With a little shock he realized he hadn't been there in weeks, even to take samples.

In the end, it appeared they weren't actually aimless and there were other things Jim wanted from life. Food for one. He guided the boat back to the shore a few miles up the coast and impressed Enzo again by getting it into a slip without the motor.

As they left the boat, the illusion of being alone and untouchable on the sea faded. As if on cue, Enzo's phone vibrated. Another text from Teo about security. Enzo sent a one word acknowledgement, then shoved the phone back into his pocket as he followed Jim up the steps from the dock.

Le Poisson sat right on the water but Enzo had never approached it that way. Inside, the restaurant had a fun beach vibe, but by the time they were seated, the sun had begun to sink toward hills across the bay. Waves lapped gently just a few feet away from their table.

He and Teo went sailing sometimes. He had dinner with the crew most Fridays. He dated sometimes, when he had the time. Nothing about dinner with this man should be unique.

But sitting across from Jim on a secluded seaside patio and watching the sun set didn't feel like a casual meal with Jimbo from the temp staff.

"Relax." Jim had taken off his sunglasses. When he smiled, his eyes crinkled disarmingly at the corners. "The crew has your back. You deserve a night off."

He did, but that didn't mean he could relax.

The base of his throat felt tight. He took a deep breath and let the sea air clear the obstructed feeling in his throat.

Before he could voice any...fears? objections?...the waiter approached. After they had decided on an appetizer and entrees, he produced a wine list. The remnants of brash Jimbo melted away as he launched into a connoisseur's discussion of the options. Eventually, he remembered himself and tossed Enzo another smile. "You're my local expert. What do you suggest?"

Enzo found himself laughing, "No, no. I couldn't interfere at this point. Besides, I would be duty-bound to recommend Royal Crest."

"An excellent suggestion," the waiter agreed loyally. "However, with your entree choices I believe you will appreciate the bottle your companion has chosen." He retrieved the list and hurried away, as though afraid Enzo might change the order.

"You're obviously passionate about your wine." Enzo let the sentence dangle, not sure how to ask how a casual laborer came by the knowledge. The same way he learned to sail, perhaps. Before today, Enzo would have said Jim was the kind of guy who drank watery American beer rather than fine wine.

Jim didn't seem to catch the almost-insult, or he took pity on him. "I've lived in California all my life. I guess it was just... there? My parents always enjoyed a good pairing. They loved Abarran wines but they're hard to get in the States. I've been looking forward to sampling some new varieties, but I haven't had much chance to indulge since we've been here."

"Your parents were Abarran?"

"Yep. North and South. That's why Lori and I are here. We've both always wanted to come, and we figured we should do it now while both of us are single and before we get so far on a career-track it would be hard to take time off. So, we got work-permits and" — he spread his hands — "here we are, spending the summer in beautiful North Abarra."

"What will you do after the party?"

"Oh, we've got some cousins along the coast we'll visit and I'm sure we'll be able to pick up some more temp work." Jim made it sound easy, as though work wasn't a concern. Enzo wondered if they planned to visit South Abarra as well but before he could ask, Jim turned the subject. "What about you? You said your house has been in the family for a long time. What's it like growing up practically in the royal household?"

"I haven't known anything else. I suppose I've never thought about it like that."

"Yes, but," — Jim leaned close and lowered his voice — "what about the *powers*? I mean, until I got here, I thought the rumors about the royal family were just fairytales. But they're real. Didn't it ever bother you growing up with people who could, I don't know, set you on fire with their mind or something? I mean, the princess seems nice, but she made a mini *tornado*."

The waiter arrived with their wine, which captured all of Jim's attention and saved Enzo from having to comment. After that, the conversation turned to a discussion of Abarran sites Jim and Lori intended to visit in between jobs. Their appetizers were delivered, then replaced with entrees. The discussion moved on to Enzo's research in the National Forest, then to the marriage of Tarik, the Duke of Arles and Sander, the Duke of Roses. The north/south union of two royals had made headlines even in America.

Surprisingly, Enzo did relax.

He stayed relaxed even when discussion stayed on the royals, which might have been an area of disagreement. Jim seemed to have an odd perspective on how the royals functioned in Abarran society, but despite his heritage, he was American. He couldn't be expected to understand.

The sun dropped lower and across the bay the hillside began to glow with lights from the village. They gleamed gold against stone and stucco and the same gold dripped into the sea and reflected off the gold highlights of Jim's eyes in the candlelight.

Enzo placed his hand over his glass. "I'm good."

Jim's hand froze, the bottle of wine half-tilted in the air. "Are you sure? You've only had one glass and it's not like you're driving."

"Not tonight." But for the first time in years, he said it with a little regret. "Maybe a coffee instead."

For Jim, there must be dessert served with coffee in the American way.

Enzo declined. He had already indulged too much.

And he wasn't done. He allowed himself to drift, breathing the sea air, listening to the surf, admiring the glints of gold in warm brown eyes. He indulged himself, not with dessert, but with the promise of good Abarran wine, sugar, and coffee on Jim's lips. He tantalized himself imagining the feel of his hands in Jim's hair, his lips against the tiny, delicate lines next to his eyes.

Later, as they made their way down to the dock, he breathed in the sea air and remembered saltwater and moonlight on bare skin.

Back on the boat, Jim cast off, then put on music rather than resume the conversation. To Enzo's surprise, he chose classical guitar.

"That's South Abarran music," Enzo pointed out.

"Should I choose something different?"

"No, I like it. I was just surprised." His mother had not held with hating all things South Abarran. They were just people, she pointed out. And someday maybe the two halves of the country would reunite. Maybe Tarik and Sander's cross-border ducal marriage was the first step. Interesting that Jim liked the same South Abarran artist as Enzo, though.

You must release desire to achieve serenity. He turned Master Inigo's lesson over in his mind as they let the wind and waves carry them back toward the estate. The rich, intricate chords of classical Abarran guitar rolled over him. What control to play like that. So much passion under the control.

Complicated, like anything more than dinner with the man next to him would be.

Enzo was a man who liked to keep things simple.

Still, he thought he might need to release some desire.

Jim walked him to his door.

Enzo invited him in for an herbal tea. He didn't keep coffee.

He didn't think they would actually make it to the kitchen, either.

"You have a lot of locks." Jim's voice was husky.

"I work for the royal family." He could barely get the words out. Suddenly Jim was close, so close. He smelled of wine and coffee and sea air. Enzo gave up on the keys and turned to face him. The gold had disappeared from Jim's eyes, the soft brown bleeding to dark promise.

Enzo touched the side of Jim's face. His thumb grazed Jim's cheekbone before he stopped with his fingers resting lightly against the silky hair. The laugh lines taunted him. He wanted his lips there. He wanted to clench his fingers in that silk, to hold and control and claim. He wanted coffee and wine and sugar. He wanted salty sweat on moonlit skin.

Instead he tilted his head slightly in inquiry.

Jim's breath hitched and he reached for Enzo.

Rrrrrr.

They both jumped apart as if shocked.

Enzo slapped at his pocket and pulled out his angrily vibrating phone to check the latest message. "Hell."

"Problem?"

"Work. I'm sorry. I'll have to take a rain check. I'm needed."

"Something I can help with?" Outside the glow of the porch light, Jim's expression was lost in the shadows. Enzo thought he detected regret in the words, but the question sounded too much like helpful Jimbo for him to be certain.

"We need to move some equipment. I have to meet Teo and a few of the lads to take care of it. There's no need to ruin your night off."

"I'll come with." Jim didn't make it a question. "Never know when you might need another pair of hands. Anyway, how long could it take?"

"A while." Enzo was already headed for his own Range Rover and he didn't take time to argue when Jim followed.

"So, what's the urgency?" Jim asked after buckling himself in. "Late-night equipment shuffle. Is that normal?"

Enzo fired a quick text to Teo and Herve, then started the engine. He considered his words before answering but couldn't see any harm in explaining. "There's been a schedule change, which isn't uncommon. The Dukes of Arles and Roses are arriving tonight instead of tomorrow afternoon. Security likes to shake things up a bit, especially with their Graces." He chanced a look at Jim. "How much have you followed Abarran politics?"

"A little. Not as interesting as the wine, I'm afraid. The American press made their marriage out like some kind of fairytale, but I'm assuming there were political ramifications."

"There have been threats. It wasn't just technical difficulties that interrupted the wedding ceremony."

"Okay," Jim said slowly. "I'm not seeing the connection to farm equipment." He didn't seem concerned about what the threats might have been.

"They aren't coming via the main road. They'll be using the farm road that runs along the olive grove." One of the things an American might not understand about Abarran royalty was that most of them didn't live in heavily fortified castles or estates. Even when unified, Abarra had been a small country. Their nobility didn't attract the same threats as larger, more politically powerful countries. In addition, for centuries their powers had meant the Abarran royals were well able to protect themselves. "D'Aramitz Estate has security, but it's not like your White House with a fence all around and snipers on the roof. The road their Graces are taking is public. The week leading up to Solstice we close it at the nearest major intersections, but if you know the farm roads around here you could still access it. We discourage that by parking some larger pieces of equipment across the road. Between the roadblocks and the hills, it's pretty effective."

They rounded a corner and the Range Rover's headlights picked out a tractor in the middle of the road. One of the estate trucks was parked on the shoulder nearby. As they approached, Teo hopped out, shielding his eyes against the bright headlights.

Enzo gave a few brief taps on the horn and Teo waved and trotted toward them. Enzo rolled the window down. "Yo, Teo."

"Boss." Teo approached the window. "You brought Jim. Good, we might need him. This will be a fun game in the dark. The mechanical tarp is in a tricky place but with enough people and lights we should manage."

"What's our timeline?"

Teo looked at his watch. "Too tight. You'd think Roses' team could have given us a little more notice."

"I think the point was to not give anyone notice."

"I suppose." Teo pulled a face. "Not going to be such a great plan if we can't get the tarp moved and they're all stuck out here. Armand went through on his motorcycle. He'll make sure there are no surprises in the middle and meet the team coming around the long way. They'll start on the other side and close it back up after the convoy is through."

"I've got some utility lights in the back," Enzo said. "You take the tractor. Let us go first so we can start setting up the lights."

Teo saluted and headed for the tractor.

"What's a mechanical tarp?" Jim asked.

"An automated harvesting tool. Basically, it's a big sheet of PVC that rolls out under the trees." Teo had the tractor moving and Enzo edged the Range Rover around it, then shot down the road. "The machine cranks the tarp out under the tree, we shake the olives onto it, then it retracts and funnels the olives into the sorter. Very efficient."

They rounded another curve and the headlights hit the harvest collector. Rolled into its housing, the machine looked a little like flatbed trailer. If the flatbed was almost as long as a semi and bright yellow.

"You're kidding me." Jim sounded incredulous as they got out of the Range Rover. "When you said tarp, I pictured something you toss over your car or boat, not a major piece of equipment. That thing has to be thirty feet long and is built into its own trailer." He pulled out his phone and snapped a few pictures. "Lori's got to see this. How did they get it there even in daylight?"

Privately, Enzo wondered the same thing. The "tarp" expanded to over a hundred square meters. The machine stretched completely across the road to the fence line on either side. The hillside jutted up sharply on one side and down on the other with the only flat surface being the road. Enzo sighed inwardly. Sometimes his crew were a little too good at their jobs. But all he said to Jim was, "If they got there, we can get it out. Let's go take a look."

On close inspection, Enzo realized they were at a side entrance to the orchard only used during harvest. With a little luck, they should be able to maneuver the tractor through the gate, attach the trailer, and then pull it up the hill. In daylight, it had probably been a little tricky to get the machine across the road, but doable. In the dark, navigating the narrow road, the hill, and the fence was going to be a lot harder.

"Let's get some light going," Enzo said. "With the utility lamps in the Range Rover and the headlights on the vehicles, I think we can manage."

Before they had all the lamps out of the trunk, Teo arrived on the tractor. Another of the estate trucks followed behind and Herve jumped out with more men and lights. "Incoming dukes," he called cheerfully. "Armand and his crew are closing the road behind them."

Enzo directed them to stations with as many lights as they had until the hill was lit up like midday. Teo inched the tractor into place. Jim and two other men pushed one side of the mechanical tarp until it swung over the hitch on the tractor, then set about attaching it.

Enzo eyed the fence, the tractor, and the angle of the trailer. It would still be a tight fit, but he thought they would make it through. He waved at Teo. Slowly the tractor started up the hill. The tarp trailer swung smoothly into line behind it, clearing the gate posts by millimeters.

Enzo breathed a sigh of relief.

He glanced back toward the road where first vehicle of the ducal motorcade had just rounded the corner. There would be a minimum of five vehicles, more depending on who might be traveling with them. The pace of the large vehicles was measured and stately along the narrow country lane. The tractor continued its slow chug, angling up the hill. A quick mental calculation assured Enzo the back end of the equipment should clear the road in plenty of time.

Sure enough, the motorcade didn't even slow. The first two cars were SUVs, security details from North and South Abarra, most likely. The third car would be the new armored Peugeot commissioned especially for their controversial graces. Enzo sighed. The marriage was a good thing, but it had brought out the fringe factions en force.

As the second SUV passed where Enzo stood, his musings were interrupted by a loud clang and then an ominous scraping and clatter. He whirled around just in time to see Teo and the tractor surge forward. The massive trailer made a lurching motion, then shot back down the hill.

Enzo threw himself to the side as the heavy machinery rushed toward him. Distantly he heard shouting from the other men around him as the out-of-control trailer clipped the gate post nearest him. The impact knocked it off course. The uphill side skewed around, heading for the fence. For a minute Enzo thought that would be it, but the fence gave way under the impact. With the back end still lodged against the gate, the momentum from the hill swung the front end around like a pendulum aimed directly at the Peugeot.

The driver must have seen what was happening, because the car picked up speed, but it was obviously too little too late. Enzo scrambled to his feet, already knowing there was nothing he could do.

Seconds before impact, the rear window went down. Enzo got a glimpse of Sander's panicked face and then the trailer jerked to a stop. Or most of it did. The duke, moniker Radioflash, was obviously using his power of magnetism on the metal components of the machine. But all the lurching about had broken whatever held the tarp in place. Meters of rigid, industrial grade yellow plastic shot out of the mechanism. The tarp hit the pavement at an angle right in front of the Peugeot's wheels, sending the vehicle off the road, through the fence on the other side, and into a tree. The impact broke Sander's control, and the rest of the machine clattered after the car, obscuring Enzo's view of the occupants.

Men and women poured out of the other vehicles. A few headed for the Peugeot, but more spread out blocking off the estate workers from the scene. Most of the crew were caught outside the perimeter, but Enzo saw three, Jim and two other temp workers, on the other side of the road, just behind where the Peugeot had gone out of control. Two of the men were already backing out of the way of the dukes' security detail. Only one headed directly for the crash.

Enzo made another fast survey of the scene. Headlights and toppled utility lamps shot blinding beams at haphazard angles though the darkness. Chaos reigned. He started toward the Peugeot. The horse, the painting, Teo's texts about increased security and their current situation pointed to one conclusion, *too many accidents.*

Jim had reached the dukes' car. He had his hand on the trunk as he negotiated the hill.

The inside of the car was dark. Impossible to tell what state the occupants were in. Were Sander and Tarik injured? Was their driver, surely one of their bodyguards, unconscious or incapacitated?

Jim took another step toward the door.

Enzo thought of brown eyes and candlelight. Teo's texts. Hours away from the estate. His throat constricted. Pressure started under his breastbone and overflowed into the back of his throat like the need to burp. He kept running. He needed to be closer. He could see Jim, but he doubted Jim could hear him. As he ran the pressure built and built until finally **rrrrrrrrbbbbbbbtttttttt** bubbled out of him.

Next to the car, Jim disappeared.

Two of the dukes' men reached the scene and wrenched open the doors. Enzo could hear voices inside, thank god. He stopped at the back bumper. Tarik and Sander's people could deal with the occupants better than he could. He pulled his phone out and used the light to search the ground until he found what he was looking for. He reached down and scooped up the small green frog.

Half an hour later the scene was cleared except for the mechanical tarp and the Peugeot, which would need a tow truck. Enzo was on the way back to the estate. A good bit of musical cars had taken place so that he, Teo, and Herve were riding together.

"Assessment," Enzo barked.

An obvious silence ensued, before Teo cleared his throat. "We have to assume it wasn't an accident. I'll have the hitch examined tomorrow. The two temps are already under watch and..." he trailed off.

"And?"

"And you have...boss, are you sure that was a good idea?"

No. "Would you rather me have let him climb in with their Graces?"

Silence.

From the back seat Herve hummed a little under his breath, then sang. *"The sting of the wasp will make men fall, but nothing escapes the fly on the wall.*"

"Stop that ridiculous rhyme right now." Enzo could feel the pressure building again. He took a deep breath into his diaphragm, held it for ten seconds, then let it out slowly. "The CIA probably made that up themselves to scare people. It's propaganda. You're Royal Guardsmen. Act like it."

Herve stopped humming. "Report came back an hour ago. It's them."

The Range Rover pulled to a stop in front of the staff apartments.

Teo brooded over the steering wheel as Enzo unbuckled. "King Bastien's not going to like this. If the Americans find out..."

"And how," Enzo asked silkily, "are the Americans going to find out?"

Teo didn't answer. Enzo opened the door and got out. He poked his head back in to snap, "First thing tomorrow morning, I want to know what the Wasp and the Fly are doing on Abarran soil. I'll walk home. Good night, gentlemen."

With that he slammed the door shut and headed to the room assigned to Jim Calhoun. He used his master key to let himself in and headed straight back to the bedroom. He didn't bother searching the room. He was sure it was clean.

In the bedroom he did a quick scan of the perimeter, making sure there were no unexpected hazards or open windows. The frog had stopped its attempts to escape his breast pocket and gone still against his heart. He pulled it out and examined it.

The tiny amphibian sat on his hand like a strangely warm statue and blinked up at him.

"A South Abarran tree frog," Enzo murmured. "You're endangered, you know."

The frog didn't answer. Enzo watched it a minute longer. The eyes were never quite right. They retained some indefinable quality of human eyes, as though they really were the windows to the soul.

This one's eyes had stayed brown. Not the good-humored medium brown of ever-helpful Jimbo, and definitely not the dark gold-flecked eyes of Jim from the restaurant. No, Enzo thought he might be staring into the eyes of agent James Calhoun, one half of the most renowned CIA team currently active.

He sat the little frog in the middle of the bed and carefully let himself out of the bedroom and then out of the apartment, making sure the door was locked behind him.

Teo was right. If the American government found out what he had done, there would be consequences. Enzo wasn't too worried. With any luck, Jimbo would be back on duty in the morning. He wouldn't remember anything. They never did.

CHAPTER SEVEN

Jim opened his eyes and found himself perched on the small table next to his bed. His knees were stiff, as if he'd had his legs bent for hours, and the edge of something hard jabbed him in the butt.

"What in the actual fuck?"

He stood slowly, his quads and calves bitching the whole way, and rubbed at the impression left by the lamp stand. He needed his phone and he needed to be mobile. *ASAP.*

0945. "Nine forty-five? Shit." Jim glared at the phone. It had still been in the pocket of his white shorts, the ones he wore out to dinner with Enzo, because apparently he'd fallen asleep with his clothes on. Fallen asleep while sitting on the nightstand.

Jim closed his eyes. They'd gone to dinner, and then Enzo had been called to clear the route for the dukes of Arles and Roses. There'd been a tarp, an....extender, that's what Enzo called it, and it had gone rogue. The dukes' car had been run off the road, and...

"That's it?" Jim distinctly remembered putting his hand on the back of the Peugeot. He could still feel the glossy, warm metal. But what had happened next?

He shot Lori a quick text. *Dad's wondering what we're up to.* That was their agreed-upon code for *I've been made.*

Because that was the only logical answer.

He spent the ten minutes it took Lori to respond mentally retracing his steps. 1900 reservation, dinner over by 2130, Enzo's room at 2230. He'd checked his phone on the way so the times were correct. Phone call maybe five minutes later — not enough time for Jim to sneak in a kiss — then twenty minutes winding their way between olive trees up a road so steep they could have toppled right into the ocean.

His memory shut down before 2330. He'd lost ten hours and fifteen minutes.

"What in the actual fuck?"

His phone vibrated. *What did you tell him?*

Lori wanted to know the plan. *Shit.* Jim raked a hand through his hair. The situation was recoverable — he hoped. What was the worst thing that could happen? He could get politely escorted from the country of Abarra with a black mark on his professional record.

But if he stayed, even if his activities were limited, he might still be in place to protect the princess. Reason enough to try. He could deal with his emotions — anger, embarrassment, and had he mentioned excoriating rage? — later. *I told him we'd be home in time for dinner.* Shorthand for carry on for now. *BTW, when does Uncle Benito arrive?*

Uncle Benito, their father's second cousin once removed, who would be joining them for tonight's dinner. Lori had made the arrangements, explaining that he'd need to present himself as the owner of a forty-foot yacht and do it well enough to fool the Duke of Champagne. Benito had responded with enthusiasm.

The family must have a genetic predisposition for subterfuge.

Meanwhile, Jim had missed the morning cattle call where Enzo assigned the volunteers their tasks for the day. Had Enzo missed him? Jim could claim that, in the confusion of dukes and cars and farm equipment threatening to slide into the ocean, he'd slipped away and hiked back to his room.

But that didn't explain what had really happened. How had he lost almost eleven hours? Anger threatened to overwhelm his logical mind. Locking his jaw, he stuffed it down for later. *Later.* After he figured out what had happened and what to do about it.

He would remember getting knocked out, wouldn't he? Running his hands over his head, Jim searched for a contusion and came up clean. If he'd been tased, he'd have marks, so he stripped off yesterday's clothes and examined as much of his skin as he could see.

Nothing.

A large dose of Versed could account for the memory loss, and it could be given by injection. Jim ran his hands over his biceps and glutes. No tenderness, bruising, or other evidence of a shot.

Also, Versed wouldn't have left him sitting on a table that was barely large enough to hold a lamp.

"Okay, so, without a logical explanation, we move on to the illogical."

Illogical, like maybe getting zapped by a supo who recognized him for what he was. Although, here in Abarra, maybe the supo-theory *was* the logical answer.

"What in the actual...? Damn it."

Frustrated with the situation and even more than that, with himself, Jim headed for the shower. He must have done something, somehow, to give himself away. He'd managed to get washed and brushed and dressed in a clean pair of khakis when his phone vibrated again. It was Lori.

Hey Jimbo, the natives are getting restless. Can you run up here and give me a hand with something?

Grabbing the closest company camp shirt, Jim gave it the sniff test and pulled it on. He also strapped on an ankle holster for his Sig P365. Small, but mighty, it was the only weapon he'd brought. He'd left his larger weapons on the boat — or at home.

He'd made a mistake thinking this little excursion wouldn't require firepower. Time to stop playing around. If he'd been made, Lori had too, and now she needed help.

Jim ran across the lawn and ducked under a low-hanging bougainvillea that surrounded the side door to the main house. Lori had said she was in Princess Odile's office, and he was familiar enough with the house to take the rear staircase to the second floor.

He didn't see anyone between the entrance and the office, and found Lori seated behind an antique desk, the kind attributed to King Louis the something-or-other, with delicately curved legs that ended with stylized paws. The floor was tile and a pair of ceiling fans hung overhead.

Lori held her phone on her shoulder with her chin so she could talk and type at the same time. She paused long enough to raise a finger at Jim when he came through the door. He stopped several steps in front of the desk. The gist of her conversation indicated that she was embroiled in a debate over the ideal shade of roses the florist would use for the grand reception. "I'm sure the Royal Abernathy blooms you have in stock are quite lovely, but the princess clearly stated she preferred a deeper pink. Are you certain your supply of Beckham's Pride is too limited?"

Jim caught her eye and raised a single brow. She flipped him off and went back to typing. After a moment, she thanked her debate partner and hung up. "How's every little thing?" Her smile gave nothing away.

"I've had better mornings." Jim aimed for lightly rueful but landed with a heavy sigh.

"I guess you have." She flipped her blond bob away from her face. "I'd love to hear all about it, but we're having a bit of a do right now."

"A do?"

Her smile grew tighter. "Smookie is missing."

His mind's eye saw an enormous, somewhat crazed-looking pug ready for hanging in the gallery. "Someone stole the painting?"

"Worse. The dog."

"How long since he? She? The dog has been seen?"

Lori beckoned him closer. "The damned thing sleeps at the foot of the princess's bed, and this morning he wasn't there. The princess has been inconsolable, so I'm running point on party planning." Her phone rang again. "Go find Enzo. He's coordinating the search."

I'm sure he is.

Lori waved him off, so Jim had no choice but to find the head landscaper, a task that left him with decidedly mixed emotions. On the one hand, Enzo was an attractive man, and the dinner they'd shared, from the view of the water to the lovely Bordeaux to the entertaining conversation, had gone very well. In fact, if it weren't for an awkwardly timed phone call, Jim would have followed through with his intention of unwrapping the body underneath the loose linen shirts and trousers Enzo preferred.

Talk about finding chinks in someone's armor. Jim had been *thisclose* to seeing the real man. Instead, he'd done his best to prevent an incident that would have made relations between North and South Abarra even more difficult.

And as a reward for his trouble, he had a gut full of embarrassment and anger and an eleven-hour hole in his memory.

None of which made him want to see Enzo again, although the professional in him knew that Enzo's answer to "What happened?" could prove enlightening. Jim might not be a supo, but he knew when someone gave him the whole truth.

On his way out he took the main staircase. In the home's grand plaza entrance, a small group of people from the grounds crew were clustered over a clipboard. Jim knew them all—Soraya, Tristan, Tristan's silent partner Eli, Ronny, and Jewel—he'd gone pubbing with them in town, he'd pulled weeds with them, they'd flipped coins over mucking out the livestock yard.

But facing them after last night took some doing. Not that he had much choice. If he didn't stick to his "everything's normal" script, he might as well hang it up and go home.

"Oh hey, Jimbo." Ronny, a cute ginger who was sadly heterosexual, saw him coming first.

"Morning, y'all. What's the happs?"

Jewel waved. "Come on. We're on a Smookie hunt."

"I heard. Anyone had any luck finding the beast?"

Soraya passed him the clipboard. "Not yet. These are the territories. Pick one that hasn't been claimed yet and get busy." She softened her command with a smile, one Jim returned.

"Doesn't look like anyone's been down to the beach yet. I'll try there."

The Frogman and the Spy

"Sure," Ronny said. "We didn't think *le petite peste* would trouble himself to walk that far."

"He's done this before?"

"Are you kidding?" Ronny and Soraya laughed.

"He never gets very far from Mama and his *bonbons*," Soraya said.

Leaving them with a wave and a smile, Jim ambled in the direction of the water. He caught glimpses of various members of the grounds crew, singly and in pairs, working their way through the gardens and plazas that made up the grounds. When he reached the maze Enzo was so carefully cultivating, he came upon Herve and Armand.

"Jim, hello!" Herve's wave was friendly enough, but the sly smile he gave Armand put Jim on edge.

"Morning."

"We missed you earlier," Armand said, his long hair tousled by the breeze. "After the night you had, we wondered if you were under the weather."

"Yeah." Herve gave his friend a subtle elbow-nudge. "Thought maybe you had a frog in your throat."

Their laughter seemed excessive, and for the first time since arriving in Abarra, the CIA agent came close to breaking through Jim's affable exterior. He didn't know what he'd missed in their comments, but the mix of truth and untruth made it clear they knew something he didn't.

Since he didn't trust himself to say anything nice, he figured he wouldn't say anything at all and kept right on walking. Their laughter faded into a brief conversation, one with enough intensity Jim glanced around for a place he could hide and eavesdrop. *No luck.*

He'd reached the gravel path that led down to the dock when Enzo hailed him. *Okay, this could be interesting.* Jim slowed his pace, and the head groundskeeper strode across the grass, his loose linen trousers billowing.

"Sorry I missed your round-up this morning," Jim said, close enough to the beach to hear the steady sway of the waves.

"It's all right. Everything okay?"

Wow, if ever he'd been asked a loaded question. "Fine. Fine." Jim shrugged. "I just slept in. It's all the fresh air out here." He raised his arms, exaggerating his good feeling. "Makes me feel like a whole new man."

Enzo gave him a guarded smile, his zen-meister persona firmly in place. "Yes. The air can leave one quite...euphoric."

Now what the heck is he getting at? There was an undercurrent to Enzo's words that Jim couldn't begin to parse. "In all the confusion of last night, I didn't have the chance to thank you for having dinner with me. I hope we can do it again."

Enzo's eyes widened in...*was that surprise?* "That would be...I'd like that."

Liar. Jim kept his smile locked in place. "Welp, I'm off on a Smookie hunt. Guess you won't be assigning any chores until the wild beast is returned to his mother."

He didn't give Enzo much chance to respond before jogging down the path. Who cared if he behaved rudely. At dinner, Enzo had actually relaxed for a while. They'd had fun, dammit, and they might have had more fun if they hadn't been interrupted. Whatever had changed between 2200 last night and now more than likely had something to do with that hole in his memory.

A braver man might have just asked Enzo what happened. Hell, he'd hear the lie. He'd know if Enzo was somehow involved.

Wait.

If his working theory was that a supo had zapped him, and if his internal radar was telling him Enzo was somehow involved....

Nah.

Before he could really connect the dots, he crested the last line of dunes before the beach. One of the princess's kayaks floated just out beyond the break, its blue and white stripes bobbing in and out of the waves. Jim paused, shading his eyes with a hand to cut down the glare. He didn't see an oar. *Is it empty? Yes? No?* He squinted harder.

Something moved.

Something that could very possibly be the missing pug.

Christ on a crutch. He hit the boathouse at a run, kicking off his shoes and grabbing the first kayak he came to. An oar had been left out leaning against a tackle box so he grabbed that, too. Catching himself, he dropped everything, ripped off the ankle holster and dumped it into the tackle box. Couldn't exactly leave that lying on the beach. Before grabbing the boat, he pulled out his cellphone and sent a text to Lori.

Mayday. Pug at twelve o'clock. Hit the beach.

Out in the sand, Smookie's kayak was still in sight, and Jim waded in without even bothering to roll up his trousers. So far that dumb dog had stayed put, but if he decided to jump around, or if the kayak got caught up in a current, things could get bad fast.

As he approached the other kayak, its lone occupant gave him a low growl, the kind where the creature's top lip curls up to expose his pearly whites.

"It's okay, Smookie my boy. I won't touch you." Rather than risk traumatizing the dog any further, he grabbed ahold of the other kayak. If he could get both boats a little closer to shore, the waves would push them in, and while paddling one-handed made for slow going, he managed it.

By the time he reached the beach, a small crowd had gathered, Princess Odile in the forefront. They caught a wave and rode it almost to the sand. There, Jim gave the dog's boat a shove toward shore. At the sound of the princess's hysterical cries, Smookie stood up, every bit the conquering hero.

Jim hopped out and dragged his kayak up behind the one Smookie had just launched himself from. He was immediately bombarded by enthusiastic congratulations, primarily by the Duke of Champagne, who had to be relieved he would no longer have to weather the princess's hysterics.

"Amazing job," the duke said, pummeling Jim's back and shoulders. "Wait, you're the one I saw on the yacht."

"Yes sir, that's me." Jim attempted to distract the duke with a handshake before the man bruised his shoulder. Truth hung heavy in the duke's voice, making Jim wonder about what he thought he'd heard.

"And will your uncle be joining us for dinner tonight?"

"Thank you for remembering. Yes, he will."

"Then you must sit at the second table. Lapin, are you here? Lapin?"

Lori burst out of the crowd, her smile brighter than her white blond hair. "Yes sir?"

The duke motioned at Jim. "Make sure he and his uncle have seats at the second table at dinner tonight. I want to thank him for his bravery today."

"I sure will."

Jim had to run his hand over his mouth to cover the smirk. "Thanks."

"Of course." Lori winked at him.

The princess called for the duke, and after a moment, the royals and their assorted assistants and hangers-on headed for the house.

Jim took the reprieve to gather his thoughts. He headed for the boathouse for his shoes. It gave him a moment of solitude, which he appreciated. Besides, he'd have been hard pressed to explain why he'd stopped to buckle a handgun's holster to his ankle.

There was someone who noticed, though. One man, standing in the doorway of the boathouse.

Enzo.

CHAPTER EIGHT

The distinctive drone of the didgeridoo echoed through the air, effectively destroying the first millisecond of peace Enzo had achieved all day. His mother's gift of timing, always in the right place at the right time, was not always to the benefit of her son.

He answered his phone without checking the screen. The didgeridoo wasn't a sound programmed into his phone. He refused to ask how it was always her ringtone no matter how often he changed devices or how secure the IT department assured him each new model was. He had his ways and she had hers.

"Good morning, Mother. Have we saved the world yet?"

This greeting was sufficient to launch Zha Zsi into an in-depth discussion of the latest Planet First! campaign.

He listened with half an ear. The rest of his attention on Jim, who was heading out of sight in one of the estate's golf carts. Following him in any way whatsoever would be beyond obvious. Letting him wander about unsupervised with an actual deadly weapon strapped to his ankle was also unacceptable. Enzo had already second, third, and fourth guessed his decision to pretend he hadn't noticed. So far his options were defined by the fact that no one was ready to confront the CIA.

Just before the golf cart disappeared over the hill, Herve stepped into the drive, waving his hands. After a brief conversation with Jim, he hopped into the cart. So that was okay. Enzo let the American spy with the gun disappear while he ate his lunch and talked to his mother.

"Are you listening, my love?"

"Sorry, birthday week," he apologized.

"So soon? Ah... I sent a gift. Tell Odile I...." There was a rare moment of awkward with Zha Zsi then. "Tell the princess I wish her a very happy birthday."

"You aren't coming this year?"

"Enzo," she sounded reproachful. "Weren't you listening?"

"Yes, Mother, the dolphins."

"In *Venezuela*. I can't leave now."

"Is that an entirely safe place to campaign?" What was he thinking? Of course it wasn't. And of course that had never stopped Zha Zsi before.

"But the river dolphins, dearest. Something has to be done. Are you sure you're happy at home? We could use you here. The planet needs you."

"Busy saving the princess and her trees, maman."

"Save the world to save the princess, Enzo."

This was an old argument. Zha Zsi was a top down activist. What did any individual matter if there was no world for them to live in? Global climate change would eventually destabilize everything. There could be no peace without a healthy planet.

Enzo agreed, but he tended to think locally. The Abarran Royals were the next step in human evolution. No matter what propaganda the Ministries of Power put out, those powers weren't limited to the royals; they were spreading through the population. Enzo believed Abarran powers might someday hold the key to the survival of both the planet and the human race. So keeping Abarra whole was just as important as protecting the ozone layer and saving the river dolphins.

"So," Zha Zsi executed a conversational zig, "The Birthday. There are lots of new people, hmmm?"

"We've taken on a few temps."

"Anyone interesting this year?"

God damnit. He was going to figure out who was feeding his mother information. "They'll all be gone in a week."

"Then you must work fast."

Jim's brown eyes glinting gold in candlelight came to mind, swiftly followed by the memory of the man in the boathouse strapping a gun to his ankle. "Don't worry. I'm taking care of business."

There was a rare moment of silence on the other end of the line.

"Enzo." His mother's voice came through the speaker as clear and strong as if she were standing next to him. "We haven't talked about your father in a long time."

He frowned. Umberto da Silva wasn't a part of their lives. Mention of his father in a phone call was usually code for something bad, but something in Zha Zsi's voice gave her words extra weight today.

"I'm not expecting him to show up for the party."

"I should have told you more about him. Next time I am home..."

"Maman," Enzo interrupted, not sure whether to answer her as her son or a guardsman. "It's okay. You told me all I needed to know."

On the other end of the line, he could hear Zha Zsi moving about. There was a sound of a heavy duty zipper, then a thump, a rolling noise, and a door opening and closing.

"Zha Zsi, are you checking out of your hotel? I thought you were staying in Venezuela."

"Yes, yes. I am staying, but a lovely gentleman has told me about a town to the south where the dolphin habitat is polluted. I must go immediately."

In the background, Enzo could hear shouting and then, "Zha Zsi! Maman, is that gunfire?"

"I'm sure it is just a car, Enzo. I have to run now, but ..." her voice was lost to the sound of some disturbance in the background. For a few seconds, all he could hear was pandemonium. Then there was the sound of a car door slamming and the noises faded to the background.

"Chachi," her childhood nickname for him sounded slightly breathless. "If your father shows up, don't let him in the house. I'll call you next week. Stay safe, my son."

The line went dead.

Enzo tried twice to return the call, but it went straight to voicemail.

If his father showed up? What did she mean by that? Had she heard something about the party? Was it just a warning to be extra alert? She couldn't have meant it literally. His father hadn't *shown up* in over twenty years.

If his father actually appeared, Enzo had no intention of welcoming him home. If mention of him was Zha Zsi's way of warning him about something else...

"Yo, boss."

His thoughts were interrupted by Teo.

"Anything new?" The report that morning had been as frustrating as everything else for the past twenty-four hours. Col. De Mangoux, commander general of the Royal Guard, had gone so far as to initiate discreet diplomatic inquiries with the CIA regarding any operations in Abarra they might have forgotten to mention.

The official word on Jim was...he didn't exist. Or rather The Fly didn't exist. Jim Calhoun was obviously a real person, but the CIA wasn't claiming him.

"Still nothing." Teo gave him a grim look. "Jim and Lori check out in all the ways I would expect them to. Social media accounts. Job histories, that kind of thing. All of it fake. They're exactly who we think they are."

"That's...unfortunate." Of course the CIA had operatives in the country, but usually they were unofficially acknowledged. The United States and North Abarra were allies, after all. The fact that Jim and Lori were here and no one would admit it raised some very uncomfortable questions.

"Is this a CIA operation? Or are they working for someone else?" Teo voiced Enzo's misgivings.

"I should have put him in a jar when I had the chance."

"You shouldn't have changed him at all." Teo rarely disagreed on strategy. "Then we could have kept pretending we didn't know anything about him. Now we've asked. Now they know we know. If anything happens to him...."

"Happens to *him*?"

"If anything happens to him, we have to explain it to the Americans. King Bastien will support you as far as he can, but if anything disrupts the treaty negotiations we'll have to deal with Parliament."

"So we're just going to let him roam around free?"

Teo gave him a sympathetic shrug. "Unless he does something more overt. Bastien says to stick to him like glue until we figure out why he's here. Oh, and don't blow your cover with the princess. You know how she likes to pretend she doesn't need security."

"Great." So now he had to babysit a potentially rogue agent of unknown loyalties who had wrangled a dinner invitation with over two dozen of Abarra's most politically sensitive figures. How was he supposed to protect the royals when he wouldn't even be in the room?

CHAPTER NINE

Despite being the ringleader at the center of the royal circus, Lori found time to go for a quick walk with Jim. Dressed in khaki shorts, boots, and matching estate staff polo shirts, they headed out along the beach where the sand gave way to craggy rocks rising up above the surf. From there, isolated from the others on the estate, they relied on the combination of the crashing waves and the sound diffusing app on Jim's phone to keep their conversation private.

Lori might have agreed to a walk, but it took about three minutes for Jim to figure out she did it because she was annoyed with him.

"So explain to me how you went from *they suspect me* to rescuing that damned mutt? I mean, if they do suspect, they're likely to think you dognapped ol' Smookie just to make yourself look good by finding him."

Okay, maybe annoyed didn't go far enough. More like pissed as hell. Jim shrugged, adjusting the app's volume so he could be heard, but not overheard. "I didn't dognap Smookie. Last night after dinner, Enzo got a call—"

"You had dinner with Enzo?" A headband kept Lori's blond bob out of her face, so there was no curtain hair to shield him from her scorn.

"Yes, but—"

"Yes, but you felt the need to act like a goddamn idiot? So, what did you say over dinner that gave us away?"

"Nothing." Jim stifled the urge to take off running. Lori might be too small to catch him, but he couldn't avoid her forever. Besides, she had a stake in this too. If he'd done something that put her at risk, she was right to be mad. "Unless the guy is a mind-reader along with his various other skills, he didn't get it from me."

Lori's anger faded to exasperation. "I hope you at least got some sex out of the deal."

"Jesus." Jim raked a hand through his hair, his face flaming. "I've been over our conversation more than once, you gotta believe me, and I can't come up with anything. But" — and here came the sticky part — "I can't remember anything between about eleven pm last night and when I woke up this morning."

"So no sex?"

"Oh for god's sake, no sex. He got a call from someone about the arrival of the two dukes." Jim went on to describe the tarp and trailer fail and how the dukes' car had been run off the road. "I went along to help, and distinctly remember putting my hand on their rear fender. The next thing I knew it was morning."

Lori kicked at the crumbled rock. "Well, losing all those hours is weird, but that doesn't mean we've been found out."

As much as Jim wanted to agree with her, he couldn't. "Look, as near as I can tell, I got zapped by a supo. I can't find a mark from a taser or a lump from a head injury or a sore spot from an injection of some kind. If everyone involved thinks I'm just Jimbo from Cali, why zap me?"

"Especially when you go at them with that wide-mouthed frog grin you've got going on."

"Real helpful, sis, thanks."

Shrugging, she smirked at him. "I agree that Jimbo hasn't done anything to deserve a supo-zap, but I'm not entirely convinced we're blown. We'll just have to be careful, especially at dinner tonight." She caught her bottom lip in her teeth. "I don't think our head landscaper is supposed to attend, but there's an open seat at our table..."

She had her cell phone out before he could stop her.

"There," she said. "The second table will be you, me, Uncle Benito, a couple of non-supo royal relations, and" — her grin brightened — "Enzo da Silva."

Jim stopped and pinched the bridge of his nose. "Why?"

"Because if Enzo suspects that you're anyone but Jimbo the wide-mouth frog, we need to keep him close, and" — she jabbed him with her elbow — "because you need to have sex, big brother."

There was really no good answer to that, so Jim just kept walking.

Lori matched his stride. "Pisses me off, though, the thought that one of these assholes might have zapped you."

"They're not assholes." *Arrogant, yes, entitled, probably, but not assholes.* Jim and Lori came to a ridge where the path began a circular descent to the beach, so he paused.

Lori stopped next to him, hands on her hips, gazing out at the expanse of ocean. "We missed out on growing up here because these very same assholes can't get along. You do realize that, don't you? Mom and Dad lost a big part of their lives, and now Mom will *never* be able to return. Makes me not want to forgive them any time soon."

"Never really thought about it, I mean, Napa doesn't suck."

"Sweetie, if the best you can come up with is *it doesn't suck*" — she mimicked his deeper voice — "maybe you need to rethink your life just a little."

Jim dug his thumb into the spot on his temple where a headache wanted to sprout up. "Now's not a good time for that."

"If not now, when?" Lori gave him an uncharacteristically serious look. "Whatever. Let's go back."

The walk back to the house took longer than Jim remembered. He had something like three hours between now and dinner. Best case scenario, he'd stay out of trouble. Worst case? Well, he'd hope for the best.

Wednesday evening's "informal" dinner could have been catered by Martha Stewart. A broad plaza had been created on the lawn between the house and the stable. Everything that didn't move — hibiscus vines, palm trees, Enzo's elephants — had been wrapped with tiny white fairy lights, with larger strings of bulbs strung from corner to corner along the perimeter.

Most of the temps had been pressed into service as waiters, their official estate polos adding a touch of informality to the event. This was the informal version, the warm-up act to Saturday's grand finale. Tonight, there were only fifty or so guests, compared with the two hundred and fifty expected to dine with the princess on Saturday.

The Head Table, with seating for a dozen along one side, sat on a raised platform. Five smaller tables were set perpendicular to it, with the Second Table in the center. Everyone at the Head Table was royal, and over a glass of delightfully dry white wine, Jim identified each. He compared their known powers with his experience the night before.

No luck.

The Duke of Arles could intercept electronic communications and the Duke of Roses could move inanimate objects using magnetic force. The Princess Odile could generate wind, and her consort the Duke of Champagne could apparently tame wild beasts, if his ride on Neutron was any indication. The distinguished Duke and Duchess of Marchand were also present. He was known as the Airlifter and she as the Groundgiver. Rumor had it that their son's superpower had been channeled into art, as he was the one responsible for the glorious painting of Smookie.

None of those powers could have caused Jim's memory loss. Prince Anatole, the Duke of Estagel, sat beside the princess. Jim flipped through his mental files, unable to pinpoint his exact power. A young woman sat on the prince's other side. *Hmm...young enough to be his daughter.* Still, the prince kept a possessive hold of the woman's hand, in a manner that was clearly not paternal.

Maybe his supo gives him the stamina of a much younger man.

Chuckling at his own snide comment, Jim turned to his "uncle" Benito, who sat to his left. Benito's salt-and-pepper hair and lanky frame bore a striking resemblance to Jim's father, which played to their advantage. "Fortunate that you could join us tonight, Uncle. I believe the duke will want to talk to you about your yacht."

Benito raised his glass. "To my yacht, may she ever sail the seas in glory."

They clicked glasses, their laughing toast interrupted by Enzo's arrival.

Enzo da Silva, his dark hair combed out of his face, highlighting his high cheekbones and full lips. He wore black linen trousers and a clingy crewneck with short sleeves that ended at the bulge in his biceps.

Whatever Jim had intended to accomplish over dinner went right out of his mind.

Enzo gave them all a graceful nod and took his seat.

A pair of young women were seated next to him, across from Benito. Distant, non-supo relatives of the princess, they gave Enzo the kind of side-eyed appraisal ordinary mortals used to observe a celebrity.

Lori nudged Jim's elbow. Raising her brows at the two girls, she whispered, "He'll be trending on Twitter by morning."

Jim chuckled into his wine. Manners took over, and he introduced Uncle Benito to Enzo. If the landscaper had any doubts about their story, his polished demeanor didn't let it show. Uncle Benito took to chatting up the two girls, who were happy to get to know anyone who was associated with Enzo.

Lori set down her cell phone and tapped the table in front of her. Jim gave his sister a raised eyebrow and a "yes," while Enzo maintained his aura of mystery.

"So," Lori said, giving Enzo a blatant once-over. "What happens when an unregistered supo is caught using his power?"

Jim knocked his elbow into hers. "You know the answer. The Ministry gets involved." The glint in her eye made him suspicious of her agenda. Besides, the subject didn't lend itself to a catered dinner and fairy lights.

"Your brother is right." Enzo's normal reserve deepened to something almost forbidding.

"I was just wondering. I mean, with all the weird things that have been happening." Lori hit Enzo with her best Le Lapin smile. "Something set Neutron off in the stable that day, and while it wouldn't have taken a superpower to set Smookie adrift in a kayak, last night...well..."

Her perky expression never changed, but there was an undercurrent that made Jim uneasy. "Not the time and place, sis."

"It's all right," Enzo said, folding his hands on the tabletop. "Although I'm not sure what you mean about last night."

LIE. The words hit Jim's brain in all capitals. Lori's cellphone rattled, demanding her attention and giving him the chance to change the subject. He just needed to pull his head out of his ass and say something.

Fortunately, Benito leaned closer to them, his lanky body gone loose-limbed with wine. "My dearest Elizabeta was sorely disappointed at having to miss this evening's festivities." They'd invented an aunt and then invented a reason she couldn't join them. With Lori distracted and Enzo remote, letting Benito talk gave Jim time to figure out his next steps.

Jim might have chickened out this morning, but now he'd stick to Enzo like a sandburr until he found out what the hell was going on.

Before they heard too many of Benito's lovely Elizabeta stories — all made-up on the spot — the princess stood and tapped her knife on the side of her wineglass. "Good evening!" Her shrill greeting damped the crowd noise more effectively than the knife. "So happy to welcome all of you to this evening's festivities."

Servers started moving around the tables, setting out salad plates.

"Before we go any further," the princess continued, "I'd like to welcome the man of the hour, my hero and Smookie's rescuer, the inimitable Jim

Calhoun." She gestured rather wildly for him to stand, so Jim did, to a round of applause.

"Thank you again, Jim. You were so very brave."

The applause continued while Jim shrank into his seat. Lori had her head down, blonde hair concealing what he guessed to be uncontrolled laughter. Even Enzo rubbed his lips with the back of his hand, as if to disguise his smile.

A waiter bumped Jim's shoulder hard. Jim glanced up, and Herve grinned at him. Not a friendly grin, either. The kind that says *You're in trouble and I'm just waiting my chance.* "Here's your salad."

Herve slammed the plate down hard enough to make two of the cherry tomatoes jump off and roll across the table.

"I am so sorry." Herve corralled the offending vegetables and tossed them at Jim's plate. One landed. The other skipped off the table and onto the platform floor.

Jim was still formulating his reply when Herve deliberately stepped on the little tomato, squashing it flat. His shrug quite clearly said, "Your move."

Jim's only response was a measured stare. Yes, he had his pistol in its ankle holster and yes, he would use it if Herve did anything untoward. For now, though, he slapped that silly grin back on his face and bided his time.

Enzo followed Herve's progress with a scowl, as if he, too, planned to take up the issue of Herve's behavior as soon as possible. Lori leaned forward, her smile bright and oh, so fake. "Wonder what that asshole does in his spare time."

Jim just shook his head. He knew there was more to Herve than his hired-hand persona, which made him a person to watch, not truly a suspect. *Or was he? It was Enzo who'd come up in his initial search.*

Enzo, who now watched him with sympathy in his gaze. Jim wanted to shake him and demand to know what had happened, who had zapped him. It was his mind, damnit. Jim had the right to know.

Before he could work out a reasonable plan — because stringing Enzo up by his heels till he talked seemed impractical — Herve returned. Ignoring the rest of them, he set a slip of paper in front of Enzo. Enzo read it and pushed away from the table, sliding the paper in his pocket. "I am sorry, but I'm needed elsewhere on the estate."

Jim couldn't trust himself to respond calmly, so he kept his jaw clenched tight. Lori was going to give him shit for not coming up with a flirtatious response, but it was all Jim could do to keep from spewing all manner of inappropriate accusations.

He glanced at his sister, who was also having difficulty keeping her mouth shut. Her phone buzzed again, which gave him an excuse to ignore her.

Suited Jim just fine. His mood turned sour and as the servers returned with their main dish, he did little more than glare at his food.

He plowed through his plate of red snapper cooked with rosemary, discovering his hunger and sopping up the juices with a hunk of bread. Herve was nowhere to be seen, *and where had Enzo gone?*

Too restless to enjoy the rest of the meal, Jim excused himself. Lori gave his hand a quick squeeze, then turned her attention to Benito. Their "uncle" was in the process of promising the two young royals a ride on his yacht, which could only lead to more trouble.

The moon gave off more than enough light for Jim to follow the gravel path leading away from the house. He circled the stable, alert for any unusual noise. Nothing more than the occasional rattle and huff of a horse settling in to sleep. He came to the place where the path forked. The right fork went to the beach, and the left went toward the dormitory where the temporary workers stayed.

Beyond that was Enzo's cottage. Jim made a conscious choice to head for the dormitory first.

His feelings were a riot of personas — frustrated lover, possible assault victim, and really, really pissed off dude — but right now he needed to let his head lead. This was a perp search, and it made sense to approach it in a methodical way.

The dormitory had the same stucco exterior and red clay tile roof as the main house. Jim started off by making a slow circle around the perimeter, checking each window for anything unusual. Subdued light shone through two windows in one corner. Jim edged closer. The roller shades were pulled halfway down. Jim squatted low, fingertips on the windowsill.

Three men were in the room. Armand was hunched over a laptop, his long hair looped up on top of his head. Enzo and Teo sat at a small table littered with glasses and a bottle of red wine. They had a map spread between them, Enzo pointing at various landmarks. They spoke too quietly for Jim to hear, until Enzo suddenly smacked the map with an open palm.

"Damnit. If Umberto is anywhere near here, I want to know, and I want to know *now*."

Umberto? Umberto...Jim toggled through his mental rolodex. *Bingo!* Umberto da Silva, Enzo's father. Jim eased away from the window, and under the cover of darkness, he sent Lori a text.

Pull what you can on Umberto da Silva.

Then, his back against a cypress tree, Jim settled down to wait. Time to have a chat with Enzo.

CHAPTER TEN

Enzo took a deep breath, letting the warm air of the summer night fill his lungs. He held the breath for a count of ten, then released it slowly. He needed to meditate.

Birthday week always got under his skin. The event was a security nightmare on a good year, but he couldn't remember one this bad. His team had headed off their fair share of trouble, but they had never had to deal with American spies.

Something moved in the shadows as Enzo stepped away from the building. He took a few more steps until he reached the drive, then waited for the man to emerge from the darkness.

"Won't your uncle wonder where you are?"

Jim shrugged. "He had to head back early. He'll be talking about meeting the royals for weeks, though."

"I hope you enjoyed yourself as well."

"Sure," Jim said, "but it's mostly family left up there now. I didn't want to intrude." He paused before slipping in, "I noticed you left early, too."

"I had work. Anyway, as you noticed, it is mostly family and not the most appropriate event for me to attend. I see plenty of royals, I don't need to eat dinner with them."

"Ouch." Jim grimaced, but didn't seem to take real offense.

A burst of laughter echoed through the night and they both glanced toward the sound. Through the trees the main house glowed on the hillside. The string quartet playing through dinner had given way to pop songs from a generation ago. Enzo knew exactly the scene Jim would have left. By now the guests would all have enjoyed a good bit of Royal Crest wine. They would be scattered around the lawn and pool in groups, catching up on family gossip and telling the same stories about past misadventures they re-hashed every year.

Enzo wondered who was getting Odile's version of the time she and her sister Coralie had eluded their guards and run off to Monaco for a weekend when they were in college. They both had too much to drink and Odile accidentally set off a mini tornado in one of the casinos while using her power to try and cheat at dice.

The princesses enjoyed diplomatic immunity and no real harm had come to either of them, but that adventure and her following escapades had set a bad precedent. The princess was convinced she was universally beloved and well capable of handling any problems herself. When she established her own household, she had declared there would be no guards intruding upon the privacy of her home.

As far as she knew, she didn't have any.

The exception was birthday week when the king not only sent a highly visible regiment, but most of the guests brought their own security details.

It should have made Enzo's job easier, but birthday week always seemed to attract trouble. Usually, trouble was the natural consequence of too many powers in one place, or celebrity watchers trying to get a little too up close and personal. Every now and then there was something more sinister and targeted.

Enzo gave up on waiting for Jim to go inside and turned toward his own home. To his surprise, Jim fell into step beside him.

"It's a nice night. You don't mind if I walk with you, do you?"

"Of course not," Enzo said politely. Although, he would feel better with Jim in his own rooms, or better yet, back at the house under the watchful eye of royal security.

Jim made a scoffing noise under his breath, as though Enzo had said something else. Together, they headed away from the house and dormitory.

They passed the first few minutes in silence and Enzo found himself wondering who the real Jim was. Devastatingly attractive of course. A master spy. Intelligent. Charismatic. The temps clustered around the ever-helpful Jimbo like groupies. Did he feel authentic friendship for any of them? Was it real?

He glanced sideways. As always, his gaze went to the laugh lines. Could you play a role so well you re-shaped the landscape of your face?

He allowed himself a pang of regret for the might-have-beens. They were peers of a sort. They might have been allies rather than adversaries. Or they might have been simply the co-workers they appeared. Under other circumstances, they might have kept each other's company simply for the pleasure of it.

None of those things were possible as long as Jim was here under false pretenses.

"About last night," Jim started.

"A very pleasant meal," Enzo interrupted. "I'm sorry we had to end our evening so soon. This time of year is not good for new friendships."

"Yeah, I'm sorry about that, too. You never seem to be off duty."

"Birthday week. It's not always like this."

"I'm glad I could help out last night," Jim said. "Funny thing though, I don't remember getting home."

Enzo tensed. The conversation at dinner should have prepared him, but he hadn't really thought it would go anywhere because this had never happened. No one ever admitted losing time.

"I remember the crash," Jim continued. "And then nothing."

Enzo resisted the urge to offer possible explanations. First rule of counterintelligence. Make your opponent do the talking.

The silence stretched. Maybe Jim had the same philosophy. Enzo forced himself to breathe.

And wait.

"I drove in with you," Jim finally said. "How did I get home?"

"With me," Enzo said. "I saw you safe inside. You were fine when I left."

The truth. Or part of it. He bit back any further elaboration.

More silence.

The sounds of the party back at the house had faded as they entered the wooded area of the estate between the main complex and Enzo's house. Ahead and to the right the boisterous sounds of the kids' campground were starting to take precedence.

"So," Jim sounded unusually hesitant. "You know almost everyone here."

Enzo made a non-committal sound. Was this a subject change?

"I thought maybe...maybe I ran afoul of one of the royals?"

He wasn't going to let this drop.

"And they did what?" Enzo asked, curious about this theory. Jim hadn't countered the story of being left safely in his room.

"I don't know." Frustration rang in his voice. "Maybe I went back out and...someone messed with my memories."

"That's illegal."

"Yeah? Well lots of things are illegal. That doesn't mean no one does them. Especially people who might think they're above the law. Who's going to stop them?"

And there it was. The CIA fell into the camp of people who thought the royals were too dangerous. Enzo swallowed. And he had potentially given one of their top agents proof of exactly what they were looking for. The implications were too far-ranging to contemplate.

He opened his mouth, to say... what, he wasn't sure...but Jim's eyes suddenly focused in the shadows among the trees.

"What's that?"

Enzo turned. At first he didn't see anything. Then he heard a faint noise from woods. He took a step closer, eyes searching the darkness.

Something moved near the base of a tree and the noise came again.

"Hello?" He strode forward, Jim at his elbow. Even searching the ground, he barely kept from tripping over the figure on the ground. The man's fatigues blended into the undergrowth. Only the glint of moonlight on his spectacles saved him. That and his rumbling snore.

Enzo dropped to his knees and shook the man roughly. "Hey there, wake up."

The only response was a louder snore.

"That's one of the king's guard," Jim said from behind him. "What's he doing out here?"

"Guarding," Enzo said shortly. He peered at the name sewn onto the uniform and gave him another shake. "Baptiste! Attention! Report, soldier!"

"Poor bastard," Jim said. "Just like me."

"Hardly," Enzo muttered.

"How do you—"

Whatever Jim was about to say was cut off as a scream echoed through the woods.

The kids.

The *unguarded* kids.

"Stay with him," Enzo barked. Then he started through the trees toward the campsite. The scream was followed by a burst of laughter, which might have been reassuring if not for the incapacitated guard. He moved as quickly as possible without announcing his presence.

Jim, he was irritated to note, had not stayed put.

The campsite was only a few yards off the path here, but they were approaching from behind the yurts. Orange light from the campfire in the center of the clearing danced across the canvas walls and sent smoke and the occasional ember drifting into the sky.

They circled the clearing, keeping to the trees. A quarter of the way around they found a second snoring guard. Enzo didn't need to complete the circle to deduce the two on the other side were in a similar state.

Finally, they got a view beyond the yurts. Portable speakers pumped out a beat. A few dozen teenaged royals were scattered around the fire showing off their moves and their powers. On the left side of the fire a tiny kid in a hoodie dropped into a coffee grinder–windmill combo, then bounced up — literally *bounced up* — over the flames to two-step on the other side. The move earned him a few jeers and catcalls which were interrupted as the flames flared up transforming into a golden dragon. Half a dozen kids hit the ground screaming as the fire dragon dive-bombed them. The screams turned into hysterical laughter as the dragon passed through them. The creature made a graceful turn then shrank until it could wrap itself around the shoulders of one of the girls sitting on the far side of the fire where it disintegrated into a shower of gold glitter.

Illusion girl leaned over to the boy next to her and whispered something into his ear. He grinned and his arm shot out, and out, and out until it disappeared into one of the huge glampy yurts and came back with a plastic cup.

"Handy. This what they let the kids get up to in the woods alone?"

"They aren't supposed to use their powers unsupervised," Enzo admitted. "But they're kids. It happens."

"Flouting authority like spoiled rich kids the world over." Jim didn't sound amused.

"You never snuck out and did stuff you weren't supposed to?"

"I snuck into an R-rated movie. I sure as fuck didn't knock out *my security detail* and leave them in the woods. These kids are dangerous unsupervised."

"They're not unsupervised. Look, their parents aren't stupid. Letting them have a little freedom at events like this is supposed to head off bigger rebellions. Most of it is staged. They're allowed to have their own camping area, someone leaves a few bottles of wine out to be pilfered and the guards are in the woods in case anything goes a little too far. They're just having fun."

"Yeah. I bet those guards think it's real fun."

Jim had a point. The snoring guards gave him a bad feeling about the whole situation. Whoever had knocked them out was over the line. And the kids seemed *really* happy.

As they watched, the b-boy made another bounce over the fire, this time not quite sticking the landing and bouncing off to one side before picking up the rhythm. The kids who had hit the dirt when the dragon passed hadn't made it back on their feet and roared with laughter over his antics.

Enzo backtracked toward the tents and ducked into the one the plastic cup had come out of. As expected, he found their bootleg stash of wine. Well, almost as expected. He gaped at the sight in front him.

"A few bottles?" Jim's voice was grim. "That's a fucking cask. How much do you think they've had?"

"We're going to have to shut the party down," Enzo admitted. "This is dangerous."

As if conjured by his words, there was another scream from outside, only this one wasn't followed by laughter. Enzo rushed outside, no longer worried about being spotted. At first everything looked the same. The kid with the arms was still putting moves on illusion girl, his arms undulating like rubber bands as glitter filled the air around them. The b-boy was still bouncing, his trajectory getting wilder and wilder. Half a dozen kids were still on the ground like it was too much trouble to get up, or maybe the ground wasn't too steady. The fire was still... Enzo's head whipped around as a second fire bloomed bright, lighting up the shadows at the edge of the woods.

Next to the second fire stood a boy. His face glowed red from the flames and his eyes were wide and terrified. The flames flared higher and the branches of the tree above him went from healthy green to singed. They glowed briefly, then the sparks winked out along with the larger flame. Enzo let out the breath he had been holding. But his relief was short-lived.

The boy's eyes went wider, then he doubled over. *Too much wine*, Enzo thought. Except what poured out of the kid's mouth wasn't wine but something that looked more like a volcanic explosion — fire and molten matter. It hit the ground like a flamethrower, igniting the grass and flaring back up into the branches. Something shimmered in the air. The smoke and flames stopped rising and then began to shrink, as though encased in an invisible bubble. A girl stepped out of the trees, thin face set in concentration. The bubble began to shrink. Deprived of oxygen, the flames inside stuttered, then winked out. *Smart girl.*

Enzo and Jim headed toward the two. As they got closer, Enzo could see both their faces were streaked with tears. The girl spotted them first. Her face reflected first panic, then relief at seeing two adults approach.

The boy was too wrapped in his own misery to notice. His face was drenched in sweat and he swayed unsteadily. Without warning he heaved another avalanche of fire. The girl pivoted back into action. Up close, Enzo could see the faint shimmer of the bubble as it encased the flames. The shimmer began to shrink, then wavered and winked out. The flames flared higher with the influx of oxygen and began to spread along the ground. The girl put both hands out and a new bubble appeared. The spread halted. This time she got the bubble down to about half the size before it wavered and disappeared. Again, the flames reacted to the oxygen with a burst of new energy.

It wasn't until the fourth try that the bubble shrank far enough to extinguish the flame. She stomped on some embers still glowing on the ground then stumbled toward the boy. He backed away. "No, no. Elle, don't get near me. I don't want to hurt you."

"Come back in the clearing," she pleaded. "I'm tired. If it gets in the trees I don't think I can stop it."

The boy finally noticed Enzo and Jim. "Stay back." He hiccupped and a tiny bubble of flame exploded in the air.

If the kid got any farther into the trees they were in real trouble. The girl was obviously exhausted. Enzo kept his voice calm, the same way Master Inigo had been calm when training him. "It's okay," he soothed. "Take some deep breaths. Let's go back to the campfire where the flames won't do any damage."

The boy was breathing way too fast, obviously panicked, which would only make his powers stronger and harder to control. Without the red glow of the fire, his face had turned sickly green. Another eruption was obviously imminent.

"It's okay," Enzo said. "We're here to help."

But the boy was no longer paying any attention to him.

"Okay, kid," Jim's voice was expressionless. "Come back into the clearing and we can talk."

Enzo whipped his head around. Jim had drawn his weapon. He held it in a two-handed grip near his body. For the moment, it was pointed toward the sky, but that didn't seem to reassure the already terrified kids.

"I didn't mean to." The boy sobbed, then turned toward the trees.

Jim cursed.

Enzo didn't hesitate. He couldn't let the kid set the whole estate on fire and he damn sure wasn't going to let Jim shoot him.

The pressure built in his chest. It felt, he imagined, similar to the way the kid felt before he belched fire. Enzo opened his mouth and released his power. ***Rrrrrrrrbbbbbbbtttttttt.***

The boy and girl both disappeared, leaving behind only another tiny belch of fire.

Enzo started forward.

"Stop right there." Jim's voice was hard.

Enzo turned.

"What the fuck was that?" Jim's face was white, but the gun trained on Enzo was rock steady.

"I've got to secure the kids," Enzo said. "They shouldn't be able to use their powers, but they aren't safe from predators."

"The kids?" Jim's laugh was disbelieving. "What kids? They just disappeared. What did you do?"

"Nothing that concerns you," Enzo bit out. "Now put down the gun."

"Lie," Jim said. The gun didn't budge.

Enzo did the only thing he could.

CHAPTER ELEVEN

Jim opened his eyes in darkness. Crouched on the floor. Muscles screaming. He stifled the instinct to stretch, staying still. Looking. Listening.

The place smelled of old incense and mud. Nearby, footsteps crossed a creaking wood floor. Someone mumbled, repeating, "What a mess, a mess, an unbelievable mess."

Did the voice sound familiar? Too quiet to tell. Jim spent a moment assessing his immediate surroundings. His back rested against something solid, but space surrounded his arms and shoulders. Easing his knees forward, he soundlessly adjusted his position.

His quads sighed with relief.

The footsteps stopped. "How long will it take you to wake up, little ones? Your parents will be worried."

No response, but this time, Jim recognized the voice. *Enzo da Silva, the mad zapper.* Whatever the hell the man had done to him, Jim had every intention of repaying the favor. He lowered himself to all fours, prepared to crawl in the direction of the voice.

"All right, well, you sit here and let me go check on the other one."

Jim had just enough time to coil himself for a spring. Enzo's footsteps crossed the floor. A click and a sudden flood of light showed he'd opened a door. Jim remained in the shadows until Enzo crossed the threshold.

Launching himself, Jim hit Enzo solidly in the ribs, driving him back through the doorway. They fell, Jim catching Enzo's wrists and pinning them to the floor.

"What" — Jim dodged Enzo's attempted head-butt — "the fuck" — he squeezed the gardener's wrists hard enough to leave bruises — "did you do to me?"

Enzo clamped his mouth shut, his gaze turning distant. Whatever he'd done, he was getting ready to do it again.

"Aw hell no." To distract him, Jim planted a knee firmly between Enzo's legs, tight against the jewels.

And he kissed him. Hard.

For a moment, Enzo froze, his lips pinned together. Jim nudged his knee close enough to learn the contours of the man's package. He licked the stubborn seam of Enzo's lips, and when they relaxed ever so slightly, he dove in again.

This time Enzo kissed him back.

There's something about kissing, Jim decided, that made a man more vulnerable than standing naked in a crowded room. It was as if parting his lips allowed his soul to sneak through. He teased Enzo with his tongue, breaking through his defenses, tasting tea and earthy man. He nipped at his lower lip, tilting his head so he could go in from another angle.

Enzo met him with the same fervor. If Jim was sharing his soul, Enzo was offering his in return. They kept on until they were short of breath and rutting against each other. Enzo's body writhing underneath him felt both deadly and perfect, a tangle Jim couldn't hope to unravel. The grind of cock against knee had Jim ready to release his grasp on Enzo's wrists, which — for better or for worse — acted like a splash of cold water.

Jim released the kiss, glaring down at Enzo. "So help me god, if you zap me again I will kill you."

The threat apparently had a quelling effect on Enzo, who stilled. He met Jim's gaze, and for a flash Jim saw a reflection of his own confusion, a flash that faded before Jim could guess what it meant.

"You really are unstoppable," Enzo whispered.

"What?"

"That was your claim when we first met, and I believe you now."

Jim ground against him. "And you're about as stubborn as I thought."

"I'm just getting started." Enzo wet his lips with his tongue. "So, are you going to let me up?"

"Are you going to do that thing you do?"

"No."

Jim tightened his grip on Enzo's wrists. "Liar."

Enzo's eyes widened for a heartbeat. "I won't do anything unless my hand is forced."

"Not lying, but not good enough." Still, lying belly-to-belly was proving to be awkward, so Jim sat back on his heels, dragging Enzo with him. Enzo sat, dark eyes shooting sparks, turning and twisting his wrists to break free of Jim's grasp. "Okay, I'll let you go, but remember your promise."

Jim let go and they both scrambled to their feet. He stayed close to Enzo, so he could tackle him if the gardener made that zapping face again. The man's strength and the heat of his body had nothing to do with it.

"You were going to shoot a child," Enzo said, as if that explained everything.

"Aw hell no. I was just trying to get his attention." Jim surreptitiously rubbed his foot against the holster at his ankle. Empty. "Besides, he was gonna burn the whole place down."

A well-timed hiccup drew Jim's attention to a small bowl sitting on a table. He guessed they were in Enzo's cabin, because the room had the right mix of spare décor and serenity. Whatever was in the bowl hiccupped again, and a faint spark floated up a few inches and disappeared.

"You zapped him, too, didn't you?" Jim didn't know whether to laugh or rage at the man. Why the hell was an unregistered suppo running Princess Odile's estate? "You better start talking, and I better like what I hear."

"Go hang out on someone else's wall, fly-boy." Enzo layered the words with an uncharacteristic level of sarcasm.

Jim crowded him, glad he had an inch or two on the man in height. "Wrong, oh son of Umberto da Silva. If I hear your father's around — "

"He's here." Lori stood in the doorway. She wore all black, with no trace of her perky lapin smile. Tossing Jim his pistol, she kept hers trained on Enzo. "Umberto da Silva was seen in town at twenty-one thirty, in the company of one Herve Velasco and three other men wearing estate polos."

Jim aimed his pistol at Enzo. "You ready to start talking?"

Enzo had gone pale, his expression grim. "What choice do I have when I'm caught between the wasp and the fly?"

Truth. "Not sure what you mean."

Enzo gave a bitter laugh. "I might not be as sophisticated as your usual opponents, but I'm not stupid."

"Oh for fuck's sake," Lori muttered. In Swahili, which earned her a hard glare from Enzo.

"Shut up," Jim responded, but in English.

Enzo glared at both of them.

"Come on" — Jim gestured with his gun — "you can't zap both of us at once, and if you zap one, the other'll kill you." *Lying.* "Now tell us what your father has planned."

"You seem to know more about my father than I do."

"Jesus," Lori snapped, "let's lock up this Keanu-wanna-be and move on to his—"

Her rant was interrupted by the distinctive drone of a didgeridoo, coming from the cell phone on the table near the mystery bowl. Moving slowly, Jim eased toward the table and glanced at the screen.

"Zha Zsi? Your mother? Why is your mother calling you in the middle of the night?"

Enzo's composure never faltered. "She probably wants to know if I'm really in danger or if she just had a bad dream."

Jim picked up the phone and extended it toward Enzo. In doing so, he caught a glimpse into the bowl. "Frogs?" The phone dropped from his fingers. "Where did you get those frogs?"

The didgeridoo stopped, then after a breath it started up again. "That's the boy you almost shot and his friend." Enzo tensed, as if bracing himself for their response. "That's my power. I can turn people into frogs."

TRUTH. Jim blinked. Their intel had been more than faulty, it was just plain wrong, and it very likely had them hanging in the wind. Also, "You turned me into a damned frog?" He had to force his trigger finger to relax.

"Twice." The barest hint of a smile crossed Enzo's lips and then was gone. Jim set his gun on the table and took a big step back. Shooting Enzo would feel good but would solve nothing.

Lori saved the moment by laughing. "So check me on this. You're an unregistered supo pretending to be a master of the zen of pruning but you're really, what? Laying the groundwork for your father's terrorist action?"

"No."

That one word resonated with so much truth Jim almost stumbled. Still, he needed to parse things a little closer. "So you're not an unregistered supo, or you're not working with your father?"

Enzo paused, his expression remote. "Neither."

Jim glanced at Lori. "Truth."

Okay, that gave things a whole different slant. "So if you're not unregistered, that means you're here in some official capacity. And I'm going to guess that the princess doesn't know, or it would have turned up in our research."

Lori didn't lower her gun, but her shoulders relaxed. "I can promise you there was nothing in all the levels I searched."

Jim stepped closer to Enzo, close enough to feel the heat of the man's body. He was about to roll the dice, and he could only hope he didn't come up snake eyes. "Tell me the worst thing you've ever heard about The Fly." Jim ignored Lori's choked sound of disgust and held Enzo's gaze.

"I heard that once in Yugoslavia, you dragged a laboring woman out of her home and made her give birth on the street like a dog."

Keeping a blank expression took every ounce of his skill. He'd dragged the fake midwife out because she was a stone cold killer, and he had good intelligence that she planned to suffocate the baby before the little thing took its first breath and then do the mother. "Do I look like the kind of person who would do that?"

Enzo dropped his gaze. "No."

Truth.

Relief infused him with confidence. "So, if you're a registered but unrecognized supo, I'm guessing that you're connected to Abarran security."

"Possibly," Enzo said, and for once, he managed to leave Jim's extra sense confused.

"Awesome." Jim covered up his uncertainty with his widest goofball grin. "We should be working together."

The phone started up its weird drone and Enzo sighed. "I welcome the Wasp and the Fly to my team, but if you'll excuse me, she won't give up until I answer."

Jim holstered his gun, looking everywhere but at the bullfrog and the smaller toad sitting in the bowl. "Tell Mom I said hi."

Heading for the door, he pointed past Lori, who grumbled but followed him out. "You need to let things go, big brother," she hissed.

Stopping when he thought they were far enough away that Enzo wouldn't hear, Jim turned to his sister. "The Wasp and the Fly. I really hate those names." He took hold of her shoulder. "I'm just grateful he couldn't come up with anything worse than Yugoslavia."

"What's done is done. Stop abusing yourself." She gave him a searching look. "More importantly, are you seriously going to trust a dude who turned you into a frog?"

"Twice," Jim said with a bitter laugh. Yes, he was still angry, but he did understand how necessity forced a man to make unpleasant choices. He also very much wanted to find himself back on top of Enzo da Silva before all was said and done.

The next morning Jim barely made it on time for Enzo's huddle. The crowd had grown by a couple of new faces and Jim forced his bleary brain to commit them to memory. He'd missed his morning cup of coffee, so when Enzo singled him out, Jim fought a scowl.

"You're with me," Enzo said, before dismissing the rest of the crew. Blinking against the brisk early-morning breeze, Jim followed Enzo on the path that led to the beach.

Halfway there, they were joined by Teo, Herve, and Armand. "Jim, I would like you to meet my compatriots. We represent the Royal Guard, and we've been charged by King Bastien to keep the Princess Odile safe without letting her know what we're about."

Okay, so he's in deeper than just "Abarran security." Enzo kept walking, so Jim stumbled after him, ignoring the others' stares.

"Calling le Lapin away from the princess would have drawn attention to us, so I trust you'll relay the information to her," Enzo said.

"You're dragging her into things too?" Herve bleated.

Jim laughed at that. "She's a better shot than any of you and she's in the princess's back pocket. Who better?"

"I did consider that." Enzo ambled on, the rest of them shuffling behind. When they reached the beach, Enzo stopped. "Today will be the busiest in terms of arrivals. We need to make a plan."

"Do you have new information?" Jim asked, squinting into the morning glare. *Or a good reason for keeping Herve close after he was seen with your father?*

"Did you notice the new faces amongst our volunteers?" Teo answered Jim's question with one of his own.

"No," Jim gave them a shadow of his foolish grin.

"There were three." Enzo's glare poked holes in Jim's lie, calling him out.

Jim rolled his eyes. "A ginger with dreadlocks, a young woman with a skull and crossbones tattooed on her wrist, and a dark-skinned blond."

Herve muttered something Jim couldn't quite hear, but the others stayed silent. Jim guessed Enzo had dragged them down here so no one could listen in on their conversation. The tide was in, waves rolling and ebbing in a steady thrum.

"I spoke to each of them," Enzo said, "and they all have plausible explanations for their late arrivals."

"But you think they're plants," Teo said.

"Yes. I have it on good intelligence that my father was seen in town last evening."

Jim wondered if Enzo had heard this from anyone besides Lori, but he kept his mouth shut.

"A little obvious for Umberto," Herve muttered.

"I agree." Enzo stared out over the breaking waves with sad eyes. "We've been operating under the premise that whoever is behind this was waiting for Saturday, for the main event, in order to make the biggest splash for their efforts."

Jim felt sympathy for Enzo's obvious conflict. "If you're father's already here, maybe they mean to strike sooner."

"Thank you." *Captain Obvious*. Jim filled in the sarcasm that Enzo had been too polite to say.

"So..." Jim met each man's eyes. "I'm aware of a few untoward events that have occurred so far. Something spooked the stallion"—Jim gazed at Herve—"and there was a near-miss with that painting." Herve couldn't hold his stare, a fact Jim filed away for later. "There was the run-away tarp trailer, and the cask of wine given to the children."

"We're aware," Enzo snapped.

Jim waved his annoyance away. "Anything else I should know about?"

Before they could respond, Jim's cell phone vibrated. He glanced down and saw Lori's message. *911 Smoke on the main campus*. "We need to go. Something's on fire." He took off at a sprint, Enzo right at his heels. The others followed more slowly, though when they were close enough to see the flames, Herve was no longer with them.

Damn.

CHAPTER TWELVE

*In...Out...*Enzo sat in padmasana and concentrated on his breath. No water. No stones. Only the breath.

The flames had turned out to be harmless, a cigarette in a trashcan on the patio. The rest of the day...*In, two, three, four. Hold, two, three, four, five, six, seven. Out, two, three, four, five, six, seven, eight. In...*

Counting breath. Even more basic.

Slowly, the day receded and the tension began to drain from his body.

Rat-a-tat-tat.

And then it came roaring back with the knock at his door.

Enzo sighed and rolled to his feet. The knock came again. The kitchen door faced the woods so it was likely someone from the estate. One of his team would have texted first. Lost guests were rare but a possibility. The last time someone had stumbled upon his home from that direction was...Enzo opened the door to find Jim on the back deck. *Not his real name*, he reminded himself. Just another alias for the Fly.

Jim moved out of the shadows. For once there was no wide smile or hearty greeting. He didn't say anything at all, just moved forward until Enzo stepped back and the spy was in his kitchen.

In his kitchen, then in his arms, hands coming up to cup his face, body crowding him against the door. He smelled of the beech forest and summer air but when their mouths met it was the sea Enzo thought of. Moonlight and salt water on bare skin. Laugh lines and ankle holsters. Secrets as deep and dark as the ocean at midnight.

"Upstairs," he managed.

They went, clumsy and fumbling.

Jim seemed just as unwilling as Enzo to draw apart. They navigated the stairs in a series of urgent kisses, frantic hands, and near disasters. They finally gained the bedroom, half naked and breathing hard. Enzo wanted light, to see everything, and dark so Jim could see nothing. He contented himself with the glow of the moon through the window, then Jim's hands found the button of his fly and light and dark didn't matter as long as their bodies could find each other.

More fumbles and tugs; more haste and less care until the remainder of the clothes hit the floor. They fell on the bed with Jim on top.

Enzo's body remembered the night before, the hard thigh between his legs, hands pinning him down. *Danger*. But his body opened, arching into the same rough pleasure.

Tonight the hands were in Enzo's hair, holding him in place while Jim's lips found his, deep and intimate. The kiss became its own kind of truth, a place of shared breath and discovery.

Is this real?

His body didn't care. The kiss was real. The hard length of Jim's cock between them was real. The hot skin against his own, the heady scent of musk, the weight of the man pressing him into the mattress.

Real.

He wrapped his arm around Jim's waist, tangled their legs together and rolled.

Jim growled in protest but didn't break the kiss. Enzo swallowed the low rumble as he snaked his hands between them to bring their cocks together.

This. This was real.

Jim was long and slender and cut. He rutted as if he were made for nothing but to give Enzo pleasure. He called out when he came and Enzo swallowed that, too. Another bit of truth.

He let his own release overtake him, Jim's hands still in his hair, face to face, tongues tangled so they breathed as one as their seed mingled in his hands.

When it was done he stilled, suspended in a moment of clarity.

You must release desire to achieve serenity.

He shifted slightly, so he could press his lips to the laugh lines at the side of Jim's eye.

Who are you?

The question seemed meaningless. Enzo rolled onto his back and let himself drift into sleep.

The vibration on his wrist brought him awake to a dark room and the realization that Jim hadn't left. Enzo listened to the even breathing from the other side of the bed. Asleep. Or good at faking.

Deciding there was no way to know, he slid out of bed. The moon had long since disappeared, but they hadn't turned out the light down the hall and it provided enough illumination for him to find his phone, which vibrated in time his watch.

He swiped the screen open, then pressed his thumb to an icon that said *grocery list*. His messages scrolled onto the screen. One from Herve. Two from Teo. The last simply said Binocular Thief. Enzo drew a breath and opened that one first.

Half an hour later, just before the first rays of dawn would be brightening the horizon at the edge of the ocean, Jim finally stirred.

He came awake fast, swinging his legs over the side of the bed, eyes scanning the room until he found Enzo. Then he stilled. His lips twitched into a smile as he took in Enzo's clothes. "Still an early riser. Want me to show you a better way to spend the morning than running or twisting your body into a pretzel?"

Enzo stood, regret already heavy in his stomach. "Don't force my hand."

"Ah." Jim reached for the pile of clothes Enzo had folded and placed on the end of the bed for him. "I thought we were on the same team, now."

"This is something else."

"What, exactly?"

"I may not be an unregistered supo, but you are. Maybe in America you could fly under the radar, but not here in Abarra."

Jim laughed. "What are you talking about?"

"Want to play Truth or Dare?"

"Okay, so maybe I'm good at picking up when people aren't telling the truth. That's not a super power, I'm just observant."

"Then you don't have anything to worry about."

"Lie," Jim muttered.

"You *probably* don't have anything to worry about." In truth, Enzo wasn't sure. Under normal circumstances, testing and registering someone was routine. Normal circumstances didn't include people with no known royal blood. Normal circumstances didn't include full-grown American spies. The king would do what he could, but outright refusing the Ministry wasn't an option. "Being an American and having family on both sides of the border might make it... tricky."

Jim stared at him. "You're kidding, right? We can't leave."

"I can't leave," Enzo corrected him. "A team from the Ministry of Powers will be here to pick you up shortly. There's nothing I can do about it."

"Lie."

"There's nothing I intend to do about it," Enzo corrected. He also had no intention of explaining that Jim was in the one place in North Abarra where the king's own guard couldn't remove him unless Enzo allowed it.

CHAPTER THIRTEEN

Jim had to work fast. On the way back to his room, he sent Lori a text saying *planting the seeds*, and he sent a second text to an associate known only as The Gnome. Using a numeric code, he requested that fake profiles for Etienne and Estelle Baroja be uploaded into the Ministerial database. That way, if anyone asked, he could prove his Abarran heritage without giving away his parents' identities.

Because no matter how long ago it had been, the governments of North and South Abarra would have something to say to a couple who dared to marry across the border.

Jim and Lori had traveled light, to get in and get out of Abarra without drawing any notice, so he'd stopped short of implanting their alternate profiles in case they left some subliminal fingerprints. *That sure worked well.* With a grimace, he let himself into his room. He didn't have a suit to change into —

there were limits to what his relatives had been able to provide for him — so a shower and a clean pair of trousers would have to do. He'd have chosen just about anything besides the estate polo shirt, but that was his only option.

His phone rang as soon as he climbed out of the shower.

"What the hell is going on now?" Lori spoke in a hushed voice, as if she were trying for privacy in a crowded room.

"Enzo alerted the Ministry to my non-existent superpower and they're on their way to bring me to a meeting in Dulibre."

Her answering stream of profanity was much less hushed. Someone knocked on Jim's apartment door, so he interrupted her. "I've made arrangements, and I'll be back as soon as I can."

She paused and he could almost hear her mind whirring. "Okay. I'll message you if anything happens, and...damn it. I'm going to dig a little deeper. There has got to be something more to our friend Enzo."

Another knock. "I've got to go."

They ended the call, and he went to greet his new friends. Two men crowded the doorway, looking for all the world like those two dudes in Men In Black.

"You're Jim Calhoun?" The Tommy Lee Jones character was the spokesman.

"I am." Most of the time. Unless circumstances required someone else.

"I'm Agent Sagari, and this is Agent Miren, and we've been tasked with escorting you to Dulibre to meet with the Ministry."

Agents S and M. Cool. Jim's nod was a shade shy of sarcasm, and he gestured toward the hallway. "Lead on."

"One minute." Agent S nodded at his partner, who came way too close to Jim for comfort. Agent M gestured at Jim to raise his arms. Jim did — grudgingly — and Agent M patted him down. Jim wasn't wearing a weapon, but the jerk did confiscate his cell phone. Jim allowed him to hang onto it because playing their game seemed like the fastest way through.

With Agent S in the lead, they headed toward their black Mercedes, a vehicle designed to intimidate with luxury. S&M took the front seats, leaving Jim alone in the rear. The drive to Dulibre took about forty-five minutes, which gave him time to think. Too much time. And no matter how often he redirected them, his thoughts came back to Enzo.

He had questions — *so many questions* — not the least of which was why the landscaper had sicced the Ministry on him. He'd honestly tried to help and look where that got him.

Jim lived his life in the shadow of secrets, so to meet an attractive, intriguing man who traded in those same shadows made that man even more desirable. And though he tried to ignore it, a little voice said a man who lived in the shadows might be less likely to judge someone else in the same circumstances.

Apparently that little voice was misguided, because Mr. Enzo *"I'll keep my secrets, thanks"* da Silva had just hung him out to dry.

Dulibre was a city; crowded, cleaner than some, its architecture a mix of classic Mediterranean and new-money glitz. Their destination was a yellow building decorated with arches over every window, the doorways framed by white Corinthian columns. With better company, the scene would have been lovely.

As it was, they assumed the same posture from the car to the meeting room, with Jim in the middle of an S&M sandwich. Imaginary-Enzo followed them in, despite how Jim needed to focus on the problem at hand.

Jim's escorts ushered him into a large, formal chamber. The sturdy table dominating the center had the heft needed to support may egos, and an array of profoundly serious people sat along one side, facing him. The man at the center sat behind a nameplate that said Minister of Powers.

Damn. Jim had studied enough to know the new North Abarran Minister of Powers didn't mess around when it came to enforcing the law.

Two women flanked him, both of them chic and slender. The other two men were older and more ponderous. Jim's assessment was interrupted when the Minister cleared his throat, pointing to the chair closest to Jim.

"Please sit, Mr. Calhoun. We have a few questions for you, please."

"Of course." Jim smiled as if he got called to the principal's office all the time. He took a seat and folded his hands on the table. "What can I do for you?"

The Minister glanced to the woman on his right. She was distinguished from the other woman by a rather severe updo pulled tight enough to widen her eyes. "We understand that you possess an unregistered superpower," she said.

"Now see? That's what Enzo da Silva said, but there must be a misunderstanding." Jim adjusted his smile to be convincing without overwhelming them. "I tried to explain to him that my family is from Abarra and I had my little...well, I hesitate to call it a talent, even. My aptitude for distinguishing a lie from the truth involves reading body language more than anything else."

He turned his palms up and widened his smile. *Nothing to see here, folks. Just an ordinary guy doing ordinary guy things.*

The Minister's gaze narrowed like he wanted to pin Jim in place. "You're sure?"

"Well, yeah, I'm sure. My parents are from North Abarra and our family name is Baroja. No royal lineage at all. Dad got offered a position at Cal Berkeley, so we emigrated to the US and several years ago, Lori and I set aside our family name for professional reasons." Which made a lot more sense than the truth, which involved a middle of the night ride over the border hidden under blankets in the back of an old farming truck.

Father had given him and Lori passports in the names Elizabeth and Michael Stephenson. That was the first time they'd used false names, but not nearly the last.

"All right." The Minister sat back, his expression deceptively blank. "Mademoiselle DuPris, if you could bring us the calibration device, we'll settle this matter."

Calibration device? Shoot.

The bun-woman stayed put, but the other rose and made her graceful way across the room. Jim honestly didn't know if his gift amounted to a power, but he'd heard vague and uncomfortable rumors about what happened to unregistered supos. Given the choice, he'd skip the calibration because he had no interest in learning whether those rumors were true.

Though it didn't seem like he'd be given the choice.

Pending the arrival of the gizmo that might decide Jim's future, the Minister leaned forward, resting his forearms on the desk. He wore his thick hair brushed straight back from his brow, the iron grey color hinting that it had once been black. "So, Mr. Calhoun, while we wait, please explain to us why you're here."

"My sister and I work in cybersecurity" — *a catchall term that covered the more benign aspects of his work* — "and we came across a rumor regarding the Princess Odile." He watched their reactions carefully. The Minister could be in the dictionary under poker face and the woman's bun was too tight to allow her expression to change, but the other two men weren't good at hiding their surprise. *Okay, so new information. Good.*

"It mighta been a little presumptuous of us, but when we saw the call for temporary workers to help out with the princess's birthday party, we figured we'd come back to our parents' home country and see if we could help."

The Minister could have been holding a royal flush or a handful of garbage. "You thought you could help? In what way?"

Jim allowed his face to relax, for perhaps the first time since landing on North Abarran soil and met the Minister's gaze dead on. "I'm a creative guy."

The woman returned, interrupting their stare-down. She carried a small leather satchel. She passed a slip of paper to the leader and took her seat. He scanned it briefly, and Jim's heart skipped a beat.

"Our records show you are really Etienne Baroja, and your sister is Estelle." He tapped the paper, his lips pressed together. "Your parents are Giselle and Xavier, and you traveled to the US in 1997."

"Like I said, we had professional reasons for the name change, and by the way, my mother passed away two years ago."

"I'm sorry for your loss," the Minister said, without a trace of regret. He opened the leather case, bringing out a small, chrome box. "Given that you've returned under less than forthright circumstances, I think we should proceed with a calibration."

Jim fought the urge to stand, wondering how far he'd get if he ran. He *really* didn't want to have his talent assessed, but he didn't have many cards to play.

"Moreau?" The Minister nodded at the burliest of his compatriots, a balding man who'd spent too much time in the gym.

Jim crossed his arms, raising his chin in Moreau's direction. *Back off.*

The man took a position across the table from Jim, blocking the rest of the room from view. He set down the chrome box. There were no lights, or wires, or buttons. For all Jim knew the test had already begun.

"Look," he said, glaring at Moreau but speaking to the room as a whole, "I am a US citizen and an agent of the CIA. If you run the test and discover I possess a power, you're not going to be able to shuffle me off to one of your containment facilities without causing an international incident."

Or at least a minor kerfuffle. *He hoped.*

The acronym C-I-A put the slightest chink in the Minister's armor. Moreau stepped aside. The Minister glared. Jim held his breath and waited. And waited. Time ticked past slower than his heartbeat.

"I've already contacted the CIA and they were in agreement with the plan." The Minister's attitude was one of complete confidence. His words, though, were a *lie.*

Jim cracked a grin. "Try again. The CIA's a damned bureaucracy. No way you got them to sign off on this without a slew of memos hitting my in-box, and meanwhile, this does nothing to protect Princess Odile."

The Minister possessed one of the best poker faces Jim had ever encountered. "What are you talking about?"

"The rumors we heard involved threats to the princess's life. That's why Lori and I came to North Abarra, and that's why I offered to help Enzo, since he seemed to be the one in charge of keeping the princess safe." Head of landscaping and officer in the Royal Guard. No wonder Enzo didn't have time for fun. "It didn't seem like he had that much help, either, despite the weird stuff going on."

He had their attention, anyway. With that in mind, Jim played his last card. "The thing is, though, I can't understand why Enzo troubled you with my story when I might have been more use to him at the princess's estate."

All five of them looked at him like he'd started talking in Russian. "I mean, look, I'm not all that, but right after I told Enzo that his father had been seen in Lesrochers, he had y'all pick me up."

He finally said something that got a reaction. All of them started blustering, but Jim just smiled. "I mean, seems odd that he called you, almost like he hoped you'd keep me busy for a while."

If the Minister's frown got any deeper, it'd leave permanent grooves in his face. "We didn't hear from Mr. da Silva directly. Someone must have noticed a note in one of his reports."

"So then his reports must also have described all the near-miss accidents and that his father has been spotted." *His father who is active in anti-royal terrorist organizations.* Jim didn't mean to throw Enzo under the bus, exactly, but the man had turned him into a frog. *Twice.*

"I'm not sure what you mean," the Minister said.

Geez. He was going to have to spell it out. "If Enzo da Silva is in league with his father, and if his father's organization is the one behind the threats to the princess, it might make sense to him to get rid of anyone who might try to stop whatever it is they're getting up to. And that would include me."

Thank goodness Lori was still there keeping an eye on things.

"Sounds like Mr. Calhoun should talk with our security people," the woman with the calibrator said. "We're really just here to track supos."

Not quite the truth. Interesting. "I'd be happy to talk to whomever, but I need to get back to the estate.

If Enzo's father is going to cause trouble, the more help the princess has, the better."

All five of them exchanged glances. "I'd hate to think," the Minister said, "that you were hinting that Enzo da Silva might be working with his father on something nefarious."

"No sir," *except I just said that very thing,* "but I am saying that I believe the Princess Odile is in danger, and if Enzo's the guy who's supposed to keep her safe, he doesn't seem to have much help."

"I'm sure he knows what he's about."

Jim dropped the smile. "Yeah, but I've been on the ground there and you hav—"

"But you make a good point," the Minister continued without letting Jim finish. "The thing I find so interesting is that Enzo knew there was danger and he sent you away. Maybe he thought they'd all be safer without you."

"You want to bet on that? Because I'd give you the same odds that he's really working with his father, and that the princess is in more danger than we know."

The Minister took another look at each of his compatriots. "Well." He sighed, a mix of frustration and weariness. "I think you should talk to our security people, and if they determine it's safe, your escorts will return you to the estate."

"But what about the calibration?" one of the men blustered.

The Ministers lips got so tight they all but disappeared. "I'll review the results after the princess is safe."

The results? Shit.

They left Jim alone while the bun woman went to request that someone from the Ministry's security division meet with him. He filed "the results" under *things to deal with maybe never*, and he sent a quick mental *thank you* to The Gnome.

He spent the rest of the time planning what he'd say whenever he saw Enzo again.

When security arrived, it was more of the same, one woman and one man, black suits, high gloss, and neither with any more personality than shoe leather. They did understand the conundrum, however. Jim described the situation from his perspective and immediately the woman summarized it.

"Either you're the threat and da Silva moved to get rid of you, or he's the threat and he wanted you out of the way."

"That about covers it."

"We'll have you return, then, but you'll be wired. We'll listen to every word you say, every cough and every snort and every fart. We'll be listening to everything you hear, as well, and if you're in range when Mr. da Silva senior arrives, we'll know that too, and we'll coordinate with the Royal Guard so they're in place to protect the princess if and when that's necessary."

Jim grinned. *Now things were getting interesting.* "I am happy to help. Abarra is my family's home, after all."

Happy to help, and happy to stick to Enzo like a frog on a lily pad. Lori might tease him about his unremarkable sex life, but there were few men who understood Jim's need for secrecy.

Until Enzo, he'd never met someone who could match him, secret for secret.

Very intriguing.

And hot.

Yeah, he should still be furious for being thrown into this quagmire, but unraveling Enzo had Jim by the balls. So, he'd play the role of the Ministry's mole. Enzo might not be up to anything nefarious, but someone was, and the security division of the North Abarran Ministry had the right idea. Sneak someone in, just like a Fly on the wall.

Enzo stared at the body on the table.

His father.

Or so he was told. After over twenty-five years he wondered if even Zha Zsi would be able to make a positive ID.

"I'm sorry for your loss." King Bastien's voice was laden with compassion and sympathy.

"Thank you." Enzo didn't turn to face the king. He was still waiting to feel... *something*... but he didn't know the man on the table. Umberto hadn't been a part of his life since he was a small child. The last time he had seen him presumably would have been memorable, but he didn't remember it. He only knew the story from Zha Zsi.

The man on the stainless-steel table could have been anyone. For Enzo, the strongest corroboration of his identity was that Zha Zsi had already been at the airport when his call finally went through.

Had he hoped to someday establish a relationship with his father? He didn't think so. Zha Zsi had been sufficient as family. He had known his father had emigrated to America. He had never felt the urge to track him down either for a reconciliation or for a confrontation. He had not been tempted to use his position to gather intelligence on his absentee parent.

That seemed like an oversight now.

Suddenly the sterile room with the stranger on the table was too much. He turned and walked out, down the hall, past reception, out of the building.

King Bastien, flanked by his personal guard, followed him. "You weren't surprised he was in town."

"His name came up last night."

"But you don't know why he was here?"

"Our intelligence said he was involved with a terrorist group." A fact he should have known, and not from their resident spy. Something occurred to him. "Did you know? Was I kept in the dark deliberately because of our connection?"

"You should talk to your mother."

A convenient dodge since Zha Zsi was on a plane for the next ten hours. For the moment, Enzo was glad. He wasn't ready to have a conversation with his mother about his estranged now-dead father who was, by the way, a potential terrorist.

"We don't know how he was killed or by whom." Enzo stated the obvious. "The American spy, Jim, or whatever he is calling himself. Where is he?"

"On his way back from Dulibre," the king said. "He's been with the Ministry team all day. His sister?"

Frankly, Enzo was more likely to suspect her. He also didn't want to examine the degree of relief he felt that Jim was safely accounted for and not detained someplace they couldn't easily retrieve him. "My team had eyes on her most of the day, but there was a period when she disappeared. They found her coming back from the beach."

"Would the time have matched up?" Bastien's tone didn't give away much, but he wasn't happy.

"Hard to say without a better understanding of how he was killed, but…" Enzo thought about the dossier they had on The Wasp and his impressions of Le Lapin. "They say The Wasp never misses. If it had been a bullet or even a knife, I would advise you to bring her in, but he doesn't have a mark on him. We still have the American government to consider if we move strongly against them."

The king let out a royal snort. "I hear you have not been so reticent with The Fly."

"I didn't think he would find out," Enzo defended his actions. "He wasn't harmed, or even detained longer than it took him to recover."

"The American government might not be as understanding as I am." The king smiled slightly.

"I was eight, sir. And they were my binoculars."

"I hear the American came closest to my recovery time. There is something to be said for a man with a quick recovery time."

Enzo ignored the innuendo. The king was an inveterate matchmaker, but he couldn't be suggesting what it sounded like. Most likely he had simply gotten wind of where everyone's favorite spy had spent the night.

"I thought, perhaps, you had formed an alliance. Are you sure we can't trust them?"

The Americans had known Umberto was in town. And Jim might be able to detect a lie, but Enzo thought he had no trouble telling them. "They haven't done anything we know of, but nor have they told us the truth. Trust is a two-way street."

Bastien regarded him gravely. "You should know he blew your cover with the Ministry of Powers. When he returns, he will be wearing a wire."

Enzo stared at the king. "He what? How do you...?"

Bastien gave him a small smile. "I'm the king. I know a great many things. I will do my best to mitigate the damage, but my influence will be limited when it comes to the Ministry. Wavelength will monitor anything he transmits and I believe we can block the signal so those idiots at the Ministry don't learn more than they should, but you should still watch what you say."

Enzo didn't know what to say. Jim had said he had parents from opposite sides of the border. He had not admitted to royal blood, but the Ministry had not detained him after testing nor had Enzo or the king been forced into a confrontation with the ministry to free him. He also had not confessed to his close relationship with the American government. Where did his loyalties really lie?

Right then, Enzo was sick of all of it. North Abarra. South Abarra. International espionage and politics. All he really wanted was to bury himself in his work, his real work. He wanted to be alone in the forest or at home with his computer and his data.

For the first time in years, he considered it. If Princess Odile got wind of his role in the Royal Guard, he wouldn't be of much use here anymore. The king might expect him to continue with the Guard in some other capacity, but he couldn't compel him. Enzo was a Guardsman by choice. His mother's heritage meant that he was a citizen of Abarra but not exactly a subject of the crown. He could quit.

"Take the day off," the king said, as if sensing his turmoil.

"I don't need to mourn a father I never knew." Although maybe he mourned not wanting to know him. "And it's birthday week."

Bastien didn't try to dissuade him. He was the king. He understood duty.

"As you wish, Sir Frog. I will trust you to keep my aunt safe."

On the way back to the estate, Enzo thought of Jim again. A man who had grown up divided between three countries.

Maybe it was another thing they had in common. For all he and Zha Zsi worked for the Crown and carried Abarran passports, they weren't truly Abarran. Or not only Abarran.

Unless you counted a diplomatically protected five acres between D'Aramitz Estate and the Abarran National Forest and a house that had been built before the Schism, they had no lands. They had no royal title, but they had a people. The Roma had a long history with the monarchs of Abarra. During that history, the Abarran Roma had developed powers right alongside the royals. Neither the Roma nor the monarchy had felt it expedient to reveal those powers.

Over the years the Roma inclination to travel and their reputation as free spirits had been useful to Abarra's kings on more than one occasion. It was a tradition Enzo and Zha Zsi continued and their diplomatic status remained a secret known only at the highest levels. Enzo had come very close to trading on it that morning when the Ministry had come for Jim.

Despite their close ties, Zha Zsi maintained they were outside of Abarran politics. Their loyalty held only as long as their goals aligned. So far that had been over three centuries.

CHAPTER FOURTEEN

Jim left the Ministry with a wire on his chest and his cell phone in his pocket. On the return trip, he received an encrypted email, likely generated by one of the tracers he'd placed on all the named parties involved in this little escapade. Someone had done something, but he wouldn't be able to open the message till he got back to his laptop.

Agents S and M kept up a stoic silence, which didn't give him much to work with. The wire — really a small black box with a slender microphone coming from the top — had been stuck to his chest with wide strips of thick, flesh-colored tape. It was going to be a bitch and a half to get off. His eyes watered at the thought.

The thing transmitted via a cellular network, so Agents S and M would be staying in the closest town to the princess's estate, Lesrochers. If Jim said anything they deemed inappropriate, they'd know where to find him.

Pocketing his phone, Jim rubbed his eyes, gritty with lack of sleep. For a minute or two last night, he and Enzo had forgotten they were adversaries. Hell, Jim had forgotten it was all an act. Their time together had been...nice. He leaned into the leather seat and shut his eyes, savoring the memory while the deluxe black Mercedes navigated the winding roads to the princess's estate.

They set Jim free about a mile from the main house, which gave him time to decide who he needed to be once he reached civilization. It was 1710 and dinner would be served in about an hour and a half. If he ran into other temps he'd pull out his *aw shucks* Jim Calhoun persona. For Lori, Enzo, or any of Enzo's crew, he'd be the more subdued version of Jim.

But who are you, really?

That was a question he barely bothered considering. He supposed Etienne, the name on his falsified birth certificate, probably came the closest, or maybe Anthony Bennett, the name on the deed for his house in California along with most of his credit cards. His neighbors knew ol' Tony Bennett was always up for three sets of tennis followed by a glass of wine and some nibbles on the patio.

Tony was a better listener than he was a talker, both by inclination and by choice, and he aimed to keep it that way. And his real name? Being forced out of Abarra at such a young age meant Jim never had learned much about that version of himself. Before now, it had never bothered him.

"Must be something in the air," he murmured.

Traffic clogged the circular drive in front of the main house, late arrivals for the princess's birthday shebang. Teo seemed to be the guy in charge, orchestrating the drop-offs and directing volunteers to wrestle luggage. Jim dodged the chaos, slipping around the house to an uncongested side door. He wanted to check in with Lori and could only hope she wasn't as swamped as Teo had been.

Only half as swamped. Jim found her at her desk, cell phone pressed against one ear and the land line's handset pressed to her chest. "What?" she barked as soon as she saw him.

He held his finger to his lips, then tugged aside the neckline of his jersey so she could see the wire. "I had a small request, but you look too busy for me to bother you."

Her eyes widened at the reveal, but otherwise she didn't react. She adjusted the cell phone and said, "Hey, let me call you back in a minute, okay?" Swiping her thumb across the screen, she put both phones on her desk. "It's been nuts in here today, but you've never let that bother you. The caterer for tonight's banquet got his numbers wrong so we only have enough fish for half our guests."

Jim stifled a laugh. "I'm sure you'll handle it."

She shrugged, her grin making it clear she understood that he had bigger things than fish to fry. "Here," she said. She picked up her phone, index finger flying over the screen. "You go make yourself useful somewhere," she murmured, her smile never faltering. "I've got a menu to revamp."

His phone buzzed before he reached the doorway. Tossing a "thanks, sis" over his shoulder, he read her text.

Target A is so clean his record had to have been wiped, and Target A's father has left the premises on a permanent basis.

That put a hitch in his step and he sent a quick response. *Dad passed his expiration date?*

Yup.

"Well now, that's an interesting wrinkle." Still mumbling, Jim retraced his steps, hoping his agenda wouldn't be interrupted. His luck held and he managed to make it to his room without running into anyone who had time to chat. He waved at a few of the other temps and dodged around a fortuitous corner when he saw Enzo in the distance.

Once in his tiny apartment, he fired up his laptop and opened the encrypted message. A familiar face stared back at him.

Herve Velasco, also known as Walter Randall Smith or Giovanni Ricci.

"Gio Ricci. That's cute." As soon as the words left his mouth, Jim remembered the wire. *Damn.* He kept scrolling, lips pressed tight. It seems that Herve held Abarran, Italian, and US passports, and was both a member of the King's Guard and a suspected associate of one Umberto da Silva. *Bingo. We've got our little trouble-maker now.*

But the senior da Silva was dead, a fact that didn't fit in any of the scenarios Jim had running through his head. He needed to know more about how da Silva died. He'd already set himself up a back door into the local police department's website, so with a few clicks and a fake log-in, he found the investigating officer's initial report.

Deceased male, approximate age 50, found face down in the water at the southern edge of Plage du

Troc. Visible injuries include superficial abrasions on his hand and face, likely from the rocks at the water's edge. Pulled from the water by the crew of a fishing boat. Wallet and identification still in his pocket. Driver's license lists his name as Rogers N. Hammerstein, a known alias of one Umberto da Silva. Awaiting medical examiner's report to verify cause of death.

Humming to himself, Jim opened a new browser page and pulled up GoogleEarth. He wanted to see the Plage du Troc. Sure enough, it was a horseshoe-shaped inlet on the north side of the princess's property with a narrow stretch of beach at the center. On either end, rocky ridges rose some thirty feet over the sand. *Did you fall in, Umberto, or were you pushed?*

Speaking aloud for the benefit of his favorite Men in Black, Jim announced he was going to change into darker clothes, then make a circuit around the plaza where the princess and her guests would be dining. "I don't know what's going down, but I have a bad feeling about this."

Wearing his darkest jeans and a black tee, Jim buckled his holster to his right leg and loaded his pistol. "I'm not going out there unarmed. No-sir-ee Bob."

Let Agent S and Agent M chew on that for a while.

He checked the time — 1812 — and headed for the door.

Enzo da Silva stood in the hall outside his rooms, hand raised as if he'd been about to knock.

"This is unexpected." Jim froze, caught completely off-guard.

"Yes, well..." Enzo shifted his weight from one foot to the other, then waved uncertainly into the room. "I have a favor to ask."

Jim eased back a step, gesturing for Enzo to come in. The man's uncertainty was so far out of character that Jim didn't know what to say. Once they were in the living room with the door closed, he gave Enzo an expectant look rather than press him with questions.

"My father is dead and I can't find Herve."

Two truths and no lie. "I'm sorry about your father."

Enzo snorted. "I'm not. I barely knew him. But Herve...."

There were a number of possible responses, but most of them should remain private. Instead of answering, Jim went to his laptop and opened a doc in a secure page. "When did you last see Herve?" Jim said, while he typed, *I'm wearing a wire.*

Enzo nodded in the direction of the laptop, apparently unsurprised. The words faded from sight.

He knew. News travels fast in a small town.

"Herve was supposed to help Teo organize the late arrivals," Enzo said, "but he hasn't been seen since lunch."

"Seems out of character," Jim said, while typing *are you asking for my help?*

Another nod at the laptop — "Herve's not the type to disappear in the middle of an assignment."

"Hmm." Jim's fingers stilled, giving Enzo time and space in case he had more to say.

Instead of speaking, Enzo pulled up a chair, slid the laptop toward himself and started typing on the blank page. *I need to know that I can trust you.*

Jim reached for the laptop, laughing softly. He couldn't hear the truth — or the lie — when someone typed the words. More importantly, if the wire was at all sensitive, the security detail could hear the clicking sound of them typing, which meant he should wrap things up.

You're asking for help. You must trust me a little. Then he paused, trying to think of something that would give Enzo the assurance he needed. His name? But which one?

He rested his hands on the keys, part of his mind balking. Enzo hadn't been exactly forthcoming either *and* he'd turned Jim into a frog. Twice. Still...

Wrestling his doubts into submission, he started to type.

Nothing written on this page will be preserved in any way. I had a false birth certificate planted in the Ministry records. The name on that birth certificate is Etienne Antton Baroja, and Jim Calhoun is the alias I use most often when I'm working.

Enzo grabbed the corner of the laptop and turned it to face him. *For the CIA?* he typed.

He looked Enzo straight in the eye and nodded once. *Yes.* Now. One more thing. One more detail to trade for trust. He rotated the laptop and typed some more.

I made my first kill at twenty-two, and my last — hopefully — at thirty. There. Shame made him close his eyes. He'd given Enzo more than anyone but Lori knew. The words disappeared and he exhaled with relief.

"I haven't called the local hospital. I suppose Herve could be there," Enzo said, then took his turn on the laptop. *You haven't mentioned The Fly.*

Jim scowled. *I really hate that nickname.* He hated everything associated with it, most importantly the things he'd had to do to earn that level of notoriety.

But you admit you're The Fly?

Disgusted, Jim spoke instead of typing. "I think we'll make more progress working together than if we each try to sort things out on our own."

"I wonder," Enzo murmured. He typed some more. *If you are The Fly, then yes, I expect we can make more progress if we work together, but I need to know who my partner is.*

"So do I," Jim said. He used the time it took to slide the laptop over to think of what it was he wanted to say. Even tired and obviously stressed, Enzo attracted him. He wanted to pour the man a hot bath and a glass of wine and Lori would *never* let him forget it if he admitted that out loud.

I could say yes, I am The Fly. Would that give you the assurance you need? Because I've already given you information that could do me a great deal of damage, and while we're in here debating, who knows what is going on at that damned dinner.

Enzo met his gaze and held it for a long moment. "Why, then? Why the charade?"

"It's like I told you. There were rumors about a threat to the princess and since Lori and I hadn't visited Abarra since we were children, we figured we'd see what we could do to help."

Enzo snatched the computer away. *It would have been more helpful if you'd come by official channels.*

With a snort, Jim took the laptop back. *Those same official channels that have a team from the King's Guard posing as gardeners?*

"We have our reasons," Enzo said.

"Well, so do I."

They glared at each other, a battle of wills that went on till Jim's eyes were burning. They only stopped when something exploded, followed by the sound of people screaming.

Jumping up, Jim ran for the door, Enzo at his heals. "Are you armed?" Enzo asked, and Jim nodded.

Yes, he was armed, and he ran toward whatever catastrophe had struck with little concern for his own safety. He was far more bothered by the words he'd shared with Enzo. The page would delete itself, but he doubted Enzo would ever forget. Jim had told a member of the King's Guard that he was CIA and given him a glimpse of his blackened soul. Enzo could kill him and be justified in doing it.

Which would be nothing compared to the international shitstorm that would kick up if Enzo told his superiors about Jim's false birth certificate.

Fuck.

By the time Jim and Enzo hit the lawn, the screams had turned to laughter. *Another near miss?* They reached the plaza, where dinner was underway. Teo and a handful of volunteers were cordoning off an area near the center where a round table sat on a raised dais.

"Something must have happened to the princess's table," Jim said, for the benefit of the Men in Black. They approached Teo, though Jim let Enzo take the lead.

"Report." Enzo's terse command earned him a side-eye from Jim, but Teo took it in stride.

"The princess's cake exploded."

"What?" Jim blurted out. The contrast between the anticipation of catastrophe and the reality of exploding cake made him laugh.

"On the center table. I mean, not her real cake. The table's centerpiece was a display of candles made to look like a cake, and right about the time she sat down, the whole damned thing blew up."

"Anyone hurt?" Enzo asked, but their attention was drawn to a burst of laughter at the edge of the plaza. King Bastien, Princess Odile, and the Duke of Champagne were making their way through the tables, shaking hands and drinking toasts with the other guests. The darling Dukes, Arles and Roses, were right behind them, along with the king's new husband, Nico.

Teo nodded at them. "They needed to clean up, but otherwise they're fine."

"That's good." Enzo surveyed the scene, arms crossed, expression grim. "I feel like someone is playing with us."

Jim had to agree. "I think it's time we take steps to get out in front of the situation."

"How do you intend to do that?" Enzo asked dryly.

"Have you seen Herve?" Jim asked Teo.

"No. Armand's gone, too."

Jim watched the royals mount the dais and return to their seats. "There was dark web chatter about an attack on the princess, but when you look at the royals seated at the table, whose death causes the most problems for Abarra?"

"Bastien, or maybe Arles or Roses, because of the animosity between the North and the South." Enzo gave Jim a calculating look. "All this could simply be a way of distracting us from their real goal."

"It could be," Jim agreed. "It very well could be."

CHAPTER FIFTEEN

The rest of the night was uneventful, if you could call babysitting a few hundred partying royals uneventful. The task was not made easier by being down two key people in a secret sub-set of essential staff.

Saturday night would be the worst, when the grounds would be open to members of the general public for music and fireworks in the evening. Thankfully, a platoon of the Royal Guard, the flashy visible kind in forest green livery, had arrived with Bastien as well as another squad of covert officers. Enzo was pretty sure there was more security around the Duke of Roses than the official count. If he were in charge of Tarik's security while he swanned off to a packed event across the border, he would damn sure have padded the entourage with a few extras the Southerners didn't know about. He just hoped their mission was limited to protecting the dukes and didn't include bonus espionage.

With all the king's men in place, Enzo was free to fret rather than patrol. At midnight, he and Jim were still ensconced in one of the small pergolas on the hillside. The location gave them a view of the grounds while maintaining a degree of privacy and featured the comfort of a small table and a couple of chairs. Jim had brought his laptop and seemed more concerned with his screen than the scene below. Whatever he was doing looked like some kind of game. He hadn't offered an explanation and Enzo didn't ask. He figured he had hit his daily cap on what Jim was willing to share.

Enzo had spent the last hour looking for any lead on Armand and Herve. He finally gave up and put the phone on the table where it couldn't tempt him to throw it.

"You need to clean house." Jim didn't look up from his laptop. "Your boy Herve has a poor work ethic."

"If you've got something, you should share."

"I just shared."

"Herve's been with me a long time." How the hell had Jim managed to wind up with a wire? Despite Bastien's promise they could block most of what he transmitted, every word had to be considered before leaving his mouth. *Most* was imprecise and not remotely the same as *all*. "He's itinerant, but he comes down for birthday week every year."

"Maybe he's got some side gigs."

Enzo turned that over in his mind, trying to decide how to respond. At least the other man wasn't sharing everything he knew with their listeners, either.

"He's always got stuff going on, but it's not like him to skip phoning in if he can't make a shift."

Jim finally closed the laptop. "He said he's Roma and he seemed to have a chip on his shoulder about working for the Royal family."

That would have been better left unsaid, but Jim couldn't know why. Enzo shrugged it off. "There have been Roma in Abarra for hundreds of years. They've never been persecuted here like they were many places, if that's what you're thinking. Herve just likes to grumble. Like I said, he shows up every summer. Anyway, it's not just Herve. Now Armand is missing, too."

He had been working with Herve for years. Jim was way off base. The most likely reason for the bitching was to gauge response to anti-royal rhetoric.

But now that the insidious thought was planted he couldn't shake it. And Jim hadn't mentioned Armand at all. Why was he so intent on Herve? "If he's not here, I don't see how he can cause trouble."

"Okay," Jim said amiably. He stretched his long legs out in front of him as he gazed down the hill. If anyone passed, he would look relaxed. Enzo distrusted the pose on principle. "Want to talk about your dad?"

"Not much to say." Umberto was turning out to be more trouble dead than he had been alive. At least he hadn't been Enzo's problem for the last few decades. The last thing he wanted was to discuss how much he didn't know about his father's recent past.

"When was the last time you saw him?"

"When I was six."

"What happened?"

Enzo hesitated. Nothing from that period could be relevant, but there was no reason not to tell the story. "I was six. Mostly I remember he wasn't home much and when he was, he yelled a lot. I suppose he and my mother were already having trouble.

"When they met, he was working for Odile and she claims he was ambitious. Zha Zsi's family had the house right next to Odile's estate. Maybe he had faulty expectations of where our association with the Royal family might lead."

If Jim had spoken, he might have ended the story there. But the other man remained silent and Umberto was dead. Maybe it was fitting to remember. "The day he left, I was here with Zha Zsi. We were weeding her flower garden. Or she was weeding. I wanted to go play in the forest." Even then, the forest had called to him. "To distract me, she told me the story of the frog prince. So then I had to find a talking frog."

He had stopped asking to go into the forest and started a frog hunt. Zha Zsi laughingly encouraged him to look under every bush in the yard. "The next thing I knew, Umberto was there. They were yelling. He grabbed her and started shaking her."

Her sun hat had flown off her head and her foot landed in the flowers as she tried to regain her balance. Funny what he did and didn't remember. "That's the last time I saw him until today in the morgue."

"Jesus." Jim was silent for a minute. "He didn't just let her go, did he?"

"I don't remember." But his mother had told him the story. His first time. The reason he had homeschooled with Zha Zsi and Master Inigo rather than going to kindergarten. "No."

"Someone's coming." Jim nodded toward the house.

Someone turned out to be Lori.

"This is what you've been doing all night? Sitting up here on your asses while the princess runs me off my feet?"

Jim grinned. "Work smarter, I always say."

Lori snorted and tossed something at Jim, who managed to catch it before it hit him right between the eyes. "What's this?"

"Bug spray."

The device looked like the kind of small battery bank you could pick up to extend your cell phone life. Sure enough, Jim plugged it into his phone. The screen flashed red three times, then green, then went black. He unplugged the device and stuck it in his pocket.

"Thanks, sis. How did you manage that?"

"Gift from the king and the Duke of Arles."

"Won't the ministry get suspicious when they don't hear anything?" Enzo interjected.

"They'll hear something, it will just be static with a few random words matched to your voice prints to keep them guessing. Wavelength was able to pinpoint the frequency so the effect is very specific. They should think their equipment malfunctioned."

"Handy," Jim said. "You've been in the thick of things. Any word on our friends Herve and Armand?"

Lori snorted. "Trust me, no one around the princess is concerned we're two gardeners short. There are so many guests here now, the Duke of

Champagne could drop off a cliff and we'd be lucky if anyone noticed."

Lori's phone made a trilling noise. She plucked it out of a pocket and stared at the screen. "Hell, I've got to get back down there. There's some kind of drama with the sleeping arrangements." She threw both of them a disgusted look over shoulder as she headed back down the hill. "Don't you boys work too hard."

Enzo watched her go.

Funny, he thought, that the Ministry had only picked up Jim. The Wasp was rumored to be an uncanny shot. He had reported his suspicions about both of them to his superiors, but only Jim had gotten the ride to Dulibre.

"How'd you convince the Ministry to let you go?"

"I let them put a wire on me." Jim's voice was wry.

Maybe. Or maybe their spy was a rare dual talent. Maybe he could not only detect a lie, but convince people to believe his own. Why else would the Ministry let him waltz out after a few cursory questions.

The combination of talents would make him an almost unstoppable spy. Or assassin.

The theory didn't stop him *wanting* to believe Jim, it just made him question his own instincts.

"We should get some sleep," he finally said. "There's nothing more we can do tonight and tomorrow will be non-stop fun."

"I'll walk you home."

Despite his misgivings, Enzo's body reacted to the husky tone.

"If you stay the night, I won't have to assign someone to keep an eye on you."

"If I stay the night, I won't have to sit out in the woods keeping an eye on you."

Enzo couldn't help himself. He laughed.

As they stood to leave, he felt a sharp sting on the back of his neck. He reached back to rub it and his fingers brushed something that felt like a tiny splinter. It fell to the ground before he could catch it. By the time his hand came away, his vision was already blurry. That should mean something, but he couldn't remember what.

Beside him, Jim slapped at his own neck.

Poison. Enzo's brain finally supplied.

"Enzo..." Jim slurred.

Or maybe it was just the echo as Enzo fell down into a well of darkness.

CHAPTER SIXTEEN

Jim had been knocked out before. Occupational hazard, really. His job was 80% scavenging the internet for clues and using what he learned to force people into awkward conversations. But 20% of the time, he got his James Bond on, and every so often that rendered him unconscious.

This was the first time, however, he'd been dragged awake by the sound of a man arguing with his mother.

"Look, Zha Zsi, I'm fine. There's nothing going on."

Jim squinted into the darkness. Enzo stood a few feet away, his silhouette highlighted by the distant lights from the piazza.

"False alarm, Mama. I'll see you when you get here." With a muttered curse, Enzo slid his phone into his pocket. Jim managed to prop himself up on his elbow, though the movement caused a sharp twinge in his neck.

"What the hell just happened?"

"My mother. She gets these feelings..."

"So I've seen." Jim sat up enough to rub at the sore spot, then pulled out his own phone to check the time. 0100. They'd lost a solid hour. "Why am I on the ground?"

Enzo squatted down close to Jim. "Tranquilizer darts."

Truth. "Darts, plural? You got shot, too?" Jim ran a hand through his hair, trying to clear the fog out of his brain. The possible reasons someone could have for knocking him and Enzo out were varied and mostly unpleasant.

"I was out for half an hour or so." Enzo shook his head. "Long enough to trigger Zha Zsi's intuition."

Jim stretched his arms overhead, not quite ready to test his legs by standing. "We should go."

"Where?"

"I'm thinking a lap around the property to make sure no one else got tagged."

Enzo stood fast enough to make Jim dizzy. "Someone would have called—"

"Not if they're all asleep."

It took Jim longer than he liked to get to his feet, and once he was there, he had to blink several times to focus his vision. Enzo gave him time, which he appreciated, but still he felt obligated to talk strategy. "Might make more sense for us to separate and keep in touch by phone."

"No."

The word landed with characteristic authority, making Jim stifle a grin. Enzo was definitely the guy in charge, and for now, Jim let him lead. "Cool. If either of us gets stung again, the other knows to drop and roll."

"Gets stung, like by The Wasp?"

Jim did a mental sidestep around the sincerity in Enzo's question. "You're joking."

Enzo gave him a long look, then headed down from the pergola where they'd been sheltered. After a moment, Jim grabbed his laptop and followed, ready to give a blustering defense of his sister. "I mean, yeah, she's capable of some pretty precise shooting, but what possible reason could she have for knocking both of us out?"

Enzo shrugged and kept walking. "I'm sure you're right, but I'd be doing a disservice to my position if I didn't entertain all possibilities."

"All possibilities." Jim shook his head, clearing away the last of the cobwebs. "We're on the same team, Enzo. You, me, *and* Lori."

Enzo didn't respond. Jim could only hope Lori's bug spray had kept the Men in Black from hearing any of that. The last thing they needed was to have Lori dragged off to Dulibre too.

Other than a pair of young royals canoodling in the labyrinth—and by canoodling Jim meant humping each other with an enthusiasm that made him blush—they didn't find anyone hanging out in inappropriate places.

They escorted the amorous pair to the young adult camp and confirmed that this time the guards were awake. Enzo's phone buzzed, stopping their forward progress while he checked a text message.

"Drama?" Jim asked. A trellis thick with grape vines, a rustling shadow in the moonlight, blocked their view of the house.

"Herve. He's at my cabin."

"That's good, right?"

"I'm not sure."

He was telling the truth, which made Jim even more curious. "Did you want me to head back to my rooms?" He hated to offer but figured they might have business that didn't concern him. *Horseshit.* He'd give Enzo a lead and then follow so he could eavesdrop.

Maybe Enzo realized that because he shook his head. "Come on. Let's go see where he's been."

They walked quickly to Enzo's cabin, the silence between them speaking of purpose and intention rather than suspicion. Jim used the time to run through possible scenarios.

Number one: Herve had used the tranquilizer darts to keep them off the board so he could set up some kind of ambush at the cabin.

Number two: basically a rehash of number one with Armand somehow assisting Herve.

Number three: ...

Nah. There weren't that many possibilities. Herve showing up right after someone knocked them out was too big to be a coincidence. "You implied Herve has other gigs. Does he have any particular specialties, skills?" Like is he a marksman?

Enzo didn't turn his head. "He's very adept at undercover work."

Neato. Herve could be working for either side. Or both.

Jim spent the rest of the walk beating himself up for getting himself and Lori into this situation with so little planning. He should never have taken on a job without having a better understanding of the situation and an actual safety net. Here, they were flying by the seat of their wazoos, and it was damned uncomfortable. Shaking his head, he followed Enzo up to the cabin.

Herve leaned against the front door. "What's he doing here?" Herve asked, nodding in Jim's direction.

Enzo didn't stop moving, forcing Herve to step aside. Without answering, Enzo opened the door and waved them both in.

"You wait outside." Herve blocked Jim's progress. "We don't need your help."

"Herve."

One word from Enzo apparently had the effect of an entire lecture, because Herve stepped aside. His glare, however, made his opinion clear.

Enzo took a seat at his dining table, staring at Herve until the man joined him. Jim waited long enough to earn a sharp nod from Enzo, and then he sat. He kept his laptop where it couldn't be seen. If they needed it, he'd bring it out.

"So we're just one big happy family now?" Herve asked.

"Where's Armand?" Enzo countered.

Herve sat back in his chair. "In his rooms, as far as I know."

"Nope." Jim glanced at Enzo for confirmation, then met Herve's glare with a deliberately banal expression.

"Where is he, then?" Herve asked.

"You always that surly or have you been saving it up for me?" Jim probably shouldn't poke the bear, but he couldn't help it.

Enzo cleared his throat. "He's been gone since before noon."

"About the same amount of time you've been missing." Enzo had asked him to stay, so Jim figured he'd make himself useful.

"I haven't been missing." Herve's snarl might have frightened a lesser man. Jim had to fight a grin.

Enzo leaned forward on his elbows, as if he could put himself physically between his quarreling compatriots. "Where were you, then? You were supposed to work the dinner tonight."

Herve's expression went blank—either surprise or preparation for a lie. Jim tightened his scrutiny.

"I told you I had to leave," Herve said. *Truth?* "Or rather, I left you a message." *Truth.*

"I never got it."

Jim tipped his head, drawing Herve's attention. "Where did you leave the message?"

Herve's blank expression grew cold. "With Armand."

Relaxing into his chair, Jim nodded toward Enzo. "He's not lying."

"Of course I'm not lying," Herve snarled.

Jim shrugged off his anger, waiting for Enzo to cue their next steps.

"You still haven't answered my question, Herve. Where were you?"

"I can't talk about it."

Jim stifled a laugh. Enzo's expression was significantly less amused. "You need to give me something or I'm going to have you arrested."

"For what?"

"To begin with, assault."

Damn, but Enzo's serious face made Jim hot. Then he remembered the wire. Pushing back from the table, he gave them his best dopey smile and patted his chest. "I'm going to give y'all five minutes or so to get this sorted, and if Herve here doesn't end up under arrest, when I get back, we should come up with a plan."

Enzo's gaze narrowed, so Jim patted his chest again, more deliberately this time. Enzo must have connected the dots because he tipped his head toward the door, and Jim left the room. He'd been ready to give Herve a fifty-fifty chance of getting arrested but lowered the odds. The guy was kind of a jerk, but he hadn't struck Jim as being devious.

He's very adept at undercover work.

Okay, so Jim would make him repeat the bullet points of whatever he told Enzo so he'd know how much of it was bullshit.

Then they needed to come up with a plan.

He made a couple laps around Enzo's cabin, senses tuned to pick up anything unusual. Their opponent—whoever they were—had created havoc but hadn't done much actual damage. Unless he counted the murder of Umberto da Silva, and possibly the tranquilizer darts tonight.

Hmm... He paused on his way back inside. So far they'd spent more time dancing around each other's secrets than they had trying to figure out who was behind all the chaos. That was going to have to change.

"Want me to slap him in cuffs?" Jim hoped his read of the room was correct. Enzo sat hunched over his elbows, brows drawn in concentration, while Herve watched him with a grin. They both blinked at Jim's jovial approach. He pulled out the chair he'd used before, spun it on one leg, and straddled it so he could face them with his hands resting on the back.

"What?" Enzo's frown showed he didn't appreciate the performance.

Jim waved at both of them. "Are you going to arrest him or did y'all work something out?"

"We worked something out," Enzo said.

"Cool." Jim pulled off his shirt, exposing the wire. "I figure if we're going to work together, we should lay our cards on the table."

Herve looked like he might take off running. "What's that?"

"Your government wants to know what I'm up to, so I'm wearing this baby for the foreseeable future."

Herve shot a question at Enzo, who sighed. "Yes, he told me. He works for the CIA but he's here for personal reasons. Is that right?"

Jim went for the wide-mouth grin. "Yup."

"To sum things up," Enzo continued, "Herve followed a lead on da Silva's killer but ran into a dead end."

"Bummer." Jim ran his fingers over the chair's polished wood.

"And..." Herve glanced at Enzo, as if he wanted permission to speak. Enzo tipped his head in acknowledgement.

"There's reason to think that one of the leaders is here, on the estate."

Jim digested Herve's words. "The leaders of what?"

"Unsure," Enzo said.

Though it might get him in more trouble, Jim decided he could come up with a partial answer for that. "In my work for the CIA, I spend time digging up info on the dark web, which is how I got twigged to the threat against the princess."

"And who made this threat?" Enzo asked, eyes narrowed in annoyance.

Jim showed him his palms. "I'm sorry for not sharing this sooner." He patted the wire. "Are y'all taking notes? Because you oughta be. This is important."

His attempt at humor fell flatter than a cement balloon, so he shrugged and kept going. "I was able to attribute the majority of the chatter to two sources. One, a shadow account run under the name of ProBarra, had a clear anti-supo bent. The posts from that account seemed to be the work of three or more people, judging from tone, word choice, and sentence structure.

"The other was the work of a single individual, someone calling themselves Royal Pain. The posts were less-frequent but more...direct. More threatening."

"And you haven't been able to identify either source?" Herve asked.

Enzo stirred, as if he meant to interrupt, and Jim stilled him with a hand on his thigh. "Given what we've learned since our arrival, I'd say the ProBarra posts were generated by the group associated with Umberto da Silva. As for Royal Pain—"

"I've heard that name," Herve said. "That's the one who's supposed to be here on the estate."

"Armand, maybe? He's still MIA."

Enzo sat with his palms together, fingertips pressed to his lips. Was he pondering Jim's suggestion? Looking for clues? Meditating on the meaning of life? Jim had no idea.

When Enzo finally spoke, he directed his question at Jim. "Is there anything else you haven't told me?"

"Yup. I like my eggs over easy and bacon instead of sausage."

Herve snorted and stood up. "I'm going back to my rooms."

"Good. In the morning I want a report on both the ProBarra and Royal Pain identities. See if you can link Armand to either of them." Enzo addressed Herve without taking his gaze from Jim.

As soon as he was gone, Jim shared one last bit of information. "I have found links between Herve and Umberto da Silva, you know."

"Good. He's supposed to maintain some level of contact with most of the known radicals in the kingdom."

Truth, or at least Enzo believed it to be true. Jim let it go. "We should probably get a couple hours sleep."

Enzo's whole demeanor changed. Instead of Serious Boss Man, he trailed his gaze over Jim's bare chest, nostrils flared like a predator scenting his prey. He stood and rounded the table, coming to rest on his knees in front of Jim.

"Say goodnight to your friends," Enzo said, his fingertips tracing the trail of hair that led from Jim's navel to the waistband of his jeans.

"Goodnight," Jim whispered, body tense as he waited to see what Enzo would do next. Enzo unzipped his fly. Jim swallowed a gasp. Maybe Lori's bug spray had interrupted the connection between the wire on his chest and Agents S and M.

But maybe it hadn't. Either way, Enzo's grin said Jim was about to find out if he could have a silent orgasm. Enzo hissed softly when he saw Jim had gone commando, and then it was all warmth and wet and solid, steady stroking. Jim's buttocks clenched and he ground his molars together. This wasn't going to take long at all.

It didn't. Not at all. If the Men in Black were curious about the high-pitched whine that had escaped from Jim's locked jaw when he came, they'd just have to wonder.

They moved to the bedroom, where Jim put Enzo to the same test. Later, as he drifted off to sleep, Jim had a surprising sense that he and Enzo together was inevitable.

Where the hell did that thought come from?

CHAPTER SEVENTEEN

Enzo woke with the nagging feeling he should never have gone to bed. It stayed with him through yoga, breakfast, and check-ins with Teo, Bastien, and his mother, who was stuck in Paris due to flight delays. She sounded serene on the phone, a benefit of knowing her powers kept her exactly where she was supposed to be.

"Chill out a little," Jim advised when Enzo disconnected the call. "Grinding on it the rest of the night wasn't going to get you anything but sleep deprivation."

"What if something had happened?"

He shrugged. "Nothing did happen. I don't know about you, but I feel a lot more capable of dealing with things after a few hours of sleep. It's not like we're in hot pursuit. We've literally got no clues."

And there was the real problem. Today was the big day and they had no idea what to expect. He went through what they knew. Chatter on the dark web, but there was always chatter on the dark web. A series of accidents that might not have been accidents. Still nothing conclusive. And then yesterday. Umberto dead. The incident with the tranquilizer darts. A clear escalation, but for what? How did everything connect?

With no answers, the only thing they could do was keep eyes on the situation and wait.

Enzo left the royal houseguests swarming the house and grounds to the uniformed guard, coordinating his own team from his kitchen table for most of the morning. Colonel de Mangoux, commander general of the Royal Guard, had set up her command station inside the house. Captain Chevalier, the head of the king's personal detail, was glued to the royal couple for the duration.

The first public events were scheduled to kick off at noon. At 11:50 Enzo finally decided he had done all he could to make sure they were ready. Now he was just an extra pair of eyes.

"What's the plan from here?" Jim asked. "Stick together or split up?"

Enzo hesitated.

"We can cover more ground if we split up," Jim answered his own question.

His brain had churned all morning, trying to find patterns. Something about the Calhouns still didn't scan. "Tell me again how you convinced the ministry to let you go."

"Look, it wasn't that hard. I told them I don't have any Royal blood and reminded them I'm an American citizen."

"That shouldn't have mattered.. Anyone of Abarran ancestry who exhibits powers falls under the Ministry's purview. Going after rogue supos in other countries is rare because of diplomatic relations, but once you're within Abarran borders you're fair game. So, tell me why they let you just waltz out."

"I told them I don't have powers. I guess they took me at my word."

"Exactly."

Jim threw him an exasperated look. "What are you so uptight about?"

"You're personable, aren't you. People like you. They tend to take you at your word a lot. Why is that?"

"You just said I'm personable."

"I didn't say you were truthful. In fact, my dear spy, you lie *a lot*. And you get away with it."

"Are we back to this? I'm sorry I didn't announce myself. This wasn't exactly a sanctioned mission. It's personal. I still want to help."

"And I want to believe you." He was sure Jim could hear the truth in his words. But did he understand the problem? Was he doing it on purpose, or did he really have no idea? "I want to believe everything you say, and I *shouldn't*. It's my job to not trust you."

"I understand that." Jim sounded...what? Like he did understand, actually. But they weren't discussing the psychological toll of having a job that made trust dangerous.

"I don't think you just detect lies. I think you can make people believe anything you say."

Jim stared at him. "You're crazy."

Maybe he was. The idea that an undocumented royal had developed not one, but two, powers and then shown up on his doorstep to *help* was pretty farfetched but...*no*. Enzo shook his head. "I'm not crazy and you're going to need to learn some control if you don't want to end up in one of the ministry's special houses."

They were coming up on the main house. A few plainclothes agents had already nodded him through and they were approaching some very visible uniformed guards.

"We don't have time for this." Jim's gaze swept the security line as if sizing up his chances. "So choose. Are we a team or are you taking me off the board?"

In the end, they split up. Enzo sent Jim to watch the royal box containing King Bastien, the King Consort, Princess Odile, the Duke of Champagne, and an entourage of other Royals and VIPs. It was a logical target. It would also be the hardest to hit since security was highest around Bastien and Odile. In terms of hedging his bets, it meant Jim would be placed where he could potentially be useful but would have the hardest time causing harm if Enzo had chosen poorly.

His own gut told him Arles and Roses were the more explosive target. The couple ignited high emotions in almost everyone. They were not only beloved by the North and South monarchs but extremely popular among Abarrans who wanted to see the countries reunited. They were just as reviled by a kaleidoscope of factions from anti-royals to separatists to personal grudge holders. An uncomfortable number of people still referred to them as Arse and The Monster. Taking out either or both of them would enflame tensions on both side of the border.

Irritatingly, the two of them had decided to skip the royal box for most of the musical performances and instead were making appearances at a variety of the side activities: judging the annual birthday cake baking contest, signing autographs for donations to the local food bank, and generally making themselves way too accessible despite the bevy of uniformed and undercover guards surrounding them.

Enzo, who had known Tarik almost as long as he'd known King Bastien, was surprised he had insisted on the meet and greet itinerary. "Arse" wasn't an entirely inappropriate nickname. The Duke of Arles was infamously devoid of tact. Apparently, he was committed to reforming his new husband's image as "The Monster" through public relations and Roses was just as determined to personally charm every North Abarran into accepting the marriage.

Enzo grabbed a crepe from one of the vendors and mingled with the crowd. He wasn't interested in getting close to Arles and Roses. Instead he hung back and scanned the people around them, looking for any potential source of trouble. Not easy when you didn't know what form the trouble might take.

As the afternoon wore on, he started to wonder if maybe all the chatter was just that, talk with no substance. The biggest excitement had been on-stage in the amphitheater when a group called Human Equality Now had managed to crash the stage. Security had removed them before they could erect a banner calling for an end to the monarchy. Enzo had monitored the whole thing through his earpiece while watching ducal security go on high alert in case the ruckus was a distraction.

Tarik and Sander had been whisked away to the main house for an hour until everything settled down. Afterward, they had taken some local children on a tour of the maze and annoyed Enzo again by calling him out of the crowd so Princess Katalin could praise the elephants.

By then the longest day was edging into evening. The Darling Dukes' entourage finally joined the other high-ranking Royals in the royal box to watch the headliners and be photographed eating cake, drinking champagne, and generally looking like everyone's fantasy of royalty. The whole thing would be capped off by a firework finale and illusion display.

Jim had managed to charm his way into the press area, as close to the royal box as he could get and not be inside. Enzo supposed he should worry about that, but the box was bristling with security and journalists had sharp eyes. Figuring the official guard had the box covered, Enzo slid into the concert crowd, keeping his eyes and ears open and hoping the tingle in his gut was wrong. Maybe they would make it through the night without incident.

On stage, the headline act had been greeted by a packed house. Out in the vendor area, the overflow crowd would be able to watch the performance on big screens. The band opened with a hit from the summer before and the crowd roared in approval. Enzo kept to the upper edges where the bowl-like design gave him the best view. He scanned the crowd, looking for counterflow — anyone focused on getting near the royal box instead of the band. All around the venue, he knew other eyes were doing the same. His earbud relayed a rollcall of terse check-ins between Colonel de Mangoux and the agents stationed outside the box. Enzo listened with half an ear. He was outside the main command chain and wouldn't need to respond unless he had something to report or one of the alert codewords sounded.

The band segued into another song and all eyes seemed focused on them. The crowd was on its feet, dancing and singing along. A few yards from where he stood, Enzo caught a glimpse of a familiar figure dancing half in the side aisle. He frowned. The Honorable Mickey Zirubri was South Abarran and had arrived with the ducal entourage. Enzo had met them at an engagement party Princess Odile had thrown for Tarik and Sander.

A lot of the younger royals preferred to be in the crowd instead of in the VIP boxes, the same way the teens preferred camping in the woods to attending the formal dinners. As the child of a baron, Mickey was hardly the highest value target present, but they were not only from the South but dating a South Abarran prince. They should be in a VIP box with security. Enzo headed closer.

Mickey was really getting into the music, but something about their dancing looked...different. As he got closer, Enzo realized Mickey's gender-changing power was activating to the beat of the music. The effect was electric and a little disorienting. Bump-bump-*male*-bump-bump-*female*-bump-bump-*male*.

The song ended just as Enzo tapped Mickey on the shoulder.

"Excuse me, uh, miss."

"Enzo!" Female Mickey beamed back at him. "Just call me Mickey. Everyone does."

"Mickey, then." Enzo glanced around. "Where's Prince Petre?"

Mickey wrinkled her nose. "Emergency assignment somewhere."

"I'm sorry he couldn't make it," Enzo said. "Weren't you given a pass to one of the VIP boxes?"

"Yes, but..." Mickey shrugged. "I feel like I'm in a fishbowl up there. Down here I can just blend in."

"The princess and her crowd can be a little much sometimes," Enzo agreed. "Was that umm... were you dancing?

Mickey blinked. "Sorry?"

"The, ummm..." He awkwardly waved his hand up and down in the direction of her body, not sure how to reference the gender flashing.

Mickey's face heated. "I guess?"

On the word "guess" their voice deepened. Before Enzo's eyes, male Mickey appeared.

He blinked a few times, face becoming softer, then more chiseled before settling into male. "I mean, not really. I seem to be out of control. Well, I'm never really in control, but nothing this extreme has happened since right after I hit puberty. Maybe the North Abarran air?"

He pushed his hair back off his face and Enzo caught a flash of red. "What happened to your arm?"

Mickey examined the single thin scratch. "Huh. I don't know. I must have brushed up against something sharp. It's just a scratch, could have been anything." ·

"Perhaps you wouldn't mind me escorting you back to your box for a while." At least until he could get a guard assigned. Mickey's wound wasn't serious enough to need a band-aid, but it was a reminder how vulnerable many of the royals could be despite their powers.

"Yeah," Mickey agreed. Their voice rose into the female range as they spoke and their body re-molded itself to match. "Maybe it would be good to cool off a little."

She sounded a little freaked, and Enzo was relieved to find their official seat was in the royal box where security was highest. He liked Mickey. As far as they knew, Enzo was just the groundskeeper. But Mickey was naturally friendly with everyone. Enzo couldn't say the same of some of the princess's other guests over the years.

He thought of Jim, who seemed just as egalitarian. Of course he had been raised in America and who knew how much of it was an act.

He escorted Mickey into the Royal box then pulled out his phone. Jim didn't have earbuds, or at least not any on the secure frequency used by the Guard.

Enjoying the band? he sent.

Not the show I expected, came back. "But sure." Jim materialized beside him.

They were in a secure breezeway at the top of the amphitheater between the royal box and the stage. "No excitement except for a few of the royals behaving like those kids the other night."

The comparison caught at the *something* Enzo's brain had been churning on. Something had been off about the kids' behavior. Before he could catch it, Jim tacked on, "entitled little snots."

He sounded disapproving. American. The tone raised Enzo's hackles. "You don't seem to have any qualms about using your own powers."

"I don't have powers," he insisted stubbornly. "Anyway, I can't hurt anyone."

"No one here would hurt anyone. That's what training is for." Again, *something*. Not an idea, but the beginning of a pattern.

"Those kids could have burned the forest down. They could have burned *themselves* down."

"That wasn't normal," Enzo snapped. He had chaperoned his share of campouts. At that age, even after a few drinks the kids didn't usually lose control. "Also, they didn't. And they're *kids*. Adults have more control." He thought guiltily of Mickey when he said it, but Mickey's power didn't hurt anyone.

And now he sounded like Jim. Whether the power could be dangerous wasn't the point. Abarrans didn't get to choose whether they were born with power.

"Yeah? Well, somebody opened some kind of magic door two feet from me and a whole family fell through it. You want to tell me that's normal around here? Where did they go? How do they get back? Maybe that's some royal punk's idea of a joke, but where I come it's an abuse of power."

Remy, Enzo thought. It had to be Remy Marchand, another of the princess's nephews. His power was a well-kept secret. Why would he have opened a door in the middle of a crowd?

"An actual door?"

"Perfectly ordinary looking wooden door. Except it appeared out of nowhere. The little girl opened it and started through. Her parents ran and grabbed her up, but as soon as they all stepped over the threshold the door disappeared."

Which sounded exactly like Remy's power and exactly *not* like Remy. Remy wanted to be a painter, not a royal. He never used his power openly and, as far as Enzo knew, no one had ever walked through one of Remy's doors without Remy. No one was sure it was possible.

He thought of the kids with their cask of wine and out of control powers.

But Remy was an adult in full control of his power. He would never be so careless.

"I'm starting to understand," Jim said, "what fuels the anti-royal factions."

Enzo didn't have an answer to that. He could say powers never got out of control and never hurt anyone. But it would be a lie.

"Sandpiper protocol." The Commander's voice over his earbud diverted his attention from the argument. This year's codewords were birds. Sandpiper wasn't a threat exactly. On the other hand, it wasn't nothing.

"What's going on?" Jim asked.

Enzo glanced back toward the box. From this angle, he had a clear view through the bullet-proof glass. "Something's happening in the box."

"Our unsub?"

"I don't think so. It could be nothing."

Jim's eyes narrowed and he followed Enzo's gaze up to the box where pandemonium reigned. The king, the princess, and almost everyone else seemed to be gesturing and running around. No one was looking at the stage. "That doesn't look like nothing."

"No one seems to be hurt." But Enzo agreed. *Something* had happened.

"Where's the king's brother?"

"Who?"

"Crewe," Jim said. "Or Krav." He gestured impatiently, "The new one."

"Prince Crave," Enzo supplied. Bastien's newly found half-brother. "I don't see him. Maybe he's sitting in the back or stepped out."

"He was standing right there a few minutes ago," Jim insisted. "I don't see him now. And no one up there is sitting down anymore. They're all clustered around the place he was standing. Any medical conditions you know about? Maybe he's sick."

As they watched, Mickey broke away from the group and ran to the front of the box. He pressed his hands against the glass and peered down.

Enzo stepped over to the rail and looked down, too. At first he didn't see anything, then noticed a minor disturbance down the side of the hill. The crowd parted a little, and he saw a young man on the ground getting to his feet. Prince Crave took a few steps back up the hill, then his foot disappeared into the ground. He lurched forward, a look of surprise on his face as though he had tripped, then he sank into the ground.

"What the hell just happened," Jim demanded. "The ground *ate* him."

"It's his power. He can travel through the earth." Enzo tried to sound calm, but his heart began to pound. Something was wrong. "We need to get up to the box."

"Why?" Jim hurried alongside him. "What's happening?"

179

"I don't know." Yet. But the *something* in the back of his brain was growing. The germ of a theory began to form. *I'm out of control.* Mickey had said. Prince Crave had looked surprised when he fell into the earth. What had Jim said earlier about some of the royals. *Like the kids the other night.* Out of control powers.

But why was it happening. And how? A new rogue supo maybe? An anti-royal or anti-Abarran supo?

More disturbances were breaking out in the crowd. An invisible force spread in a circle from one area pushing everyone out of its way until a single person was left in the middle. Enzo recognized the girl who had put out the fires with her force fields.

In another section, gravity seemed to have weakened. People bounced into the air with each step.

Ice coated one section of the hill, causing people to slide down it. In another section, fast-growing vines were covering the benches.

Enzo pulled Jim to a stop. "Did Prince Crave leave the box?"

"Yeah. Apparently he and the boyfriend prefer those long sausages the vendors are hawking over whatever's on the royal menu. Security was on them the whole time, though."

"But they left the box?" Mickey had been out in the crowd dancing. Whatever was happening was bad, but maybe security in the box hadn't been breached.

"What are you thinking?" Jim asked. He tilted his head to one side. There was still a faint mark from the tranquilizer dart, Enzo noticed.

Several things connected in his brain. Darts, the scratch on Mickey's arm, the out-of-control royals. He keyed his mike, "Recommend Lark, ma'am. I'm on my way and I'll explain when I get there."

"What's Lark?" Jim asked.

"Lockdown." Enzo explained. "I'm hoping the box is still secure. Mickey and Prince Crave were outside. Someone is drugging the royals. I think they're using tranquiller darts — something too small to be noticed by the guards."

He tried not to think about Tarik and Sander. The dukes had been out among the public most of the day. How long before the drug took effect?

Just then, the music went silent. Static hissed through the air, then a new voice blared out of the speakers. "Bas, I have to get Sander to safety."

Tarik, who would never let his power broadcast such a message publicly. If he was compromised, so was Sander, who some still called *The Monster* because he had killed multiple people in a freak childhood accident before learning to control his power.

Enzo broke into a run, Jim right behind him.

CHAPTER EIGHTEEN

Chaos reigned inside the box. Everyone seemed to be talking at once. In the middle of it all, the king was engaged in a standoff with his favorite cousin. Bastien, wisely, had followed the advice of Colonel de Mangoux and Captain Chevalier and refused to allow anyone out of the box. The Duke of Arles was having none of it.

"We need to leave now, Sander isn't safe." Tarik's voice had stopped blaring out of the speakers. The Duke of Roses had his arms around him, effectively insulating his power.

"On the contrary," Bastien replied, "the only people affected have left the box. You are safer here with me and my Guard than almost anywhere else."

Enzo hoped that was true. So far, the king was correct. But the dukes had been right here with everyone else for almost two hours. Prince Crave had gone out for his merguez frites less than half an hour ago and had already succumbed. Either the drug had wildly varying reaction times, or the royal box wasn't as secure as they all thought.

Enzo moved closer to Tarik. "With your permission, Your Grace." Tarik turned a furious face his way, only relaxing slightly when he recognized Enzo. "We believe you have been drugged. May I examine you for a wound?"

The duke nodded his approval.

The search was short. A red spot, almost unnoticeable on the back of the duke's neck with the merest pinprick in the middle where the dart had entered. Mickey's scratch had been far more noticeable.

"That's it?" Bastien's disbelief mirrored Enzo's thoughts. "Are you sure? I've never heard of a drug that could cause powers to go haywire. Isn't it more likely a rogue supo is causing this?" The king looked more distraught than Enzo had ever seen him, obviously remembering his own brush with Mastermind.

"Enzo."

He ignored Jim in favor of the king. "Sir, most of the intelligence threats we're monitoring have been from anti-supo groups. We think we're looking at an anti-supo weapon, not an unregistered power." Whatever Jim wanted could wait while they examined Sander for a dart wound. *The monster.* He hadn't thought of Sander Fiala that way since the truth about his childhood accident had come out, but if it happened again...

"*Enzo.*" The urgency in Jim's voice couldn't be ignored.

Enzo whipped his head around, leaving Tarik to search Sander for signs of a dart. But Jim wasn't looking at him. He was staring at the front of the box. Enzo turned slowly. Princess Odile had activated the PA system. Earlier in the evening, the same system had been used for her annual birthday address, a gracious thank you to the crowd for celebrating with her.

Now she was initiating an evacuation of the venue. "Everyone remain calm and return to your cars. The Royal Guard will restore order soon."

No one outside was calm. The band had disappeared. The stampede toward the exits had become an obstacle course of destruction caused by out-of-control powers. Another group of protestors had appeared, this one more effective. A giant banner hung over the stage. "POWER CORRUPTS — POWERS OPRESS — END THE MONARCHY — OUTLAW SUPOS."

Over his earbud, Teo, who oversaw estate evacuation protocols, had taken lead and was issuing a constant stream of orders.

Not good. None of it good. But the scene below wasn't what raised the hair on the back of Enzo's neck.

An unnatural breeze had kicked up in the booth. Behind the princess the air swirled with power. On the back of the royal shoulder blade, left bare by her sundress, a needle no thicker than a hair protruded. As they watched, it fell to the floor.

"We're fucked." Jim's words echoed Enzo's thoughts.

The princess hadn't left the box since she had arrived mid-afternoon. Which meant their terrorist was locked in with them.

Enzo spun, cataloguing the other occupants of the box. Most were Royals themselves or Royal spouses. The Royal Guard assigned to the king's personal retinue had the highest security clearances. Who was the traitor?

Behind him, the wind picked up. The princess's power was building. The mini tornado in the gallery had been a display of exquisite control. Enzo had no idea what she was capable of unchecked.

To his left, Tarik let out a shocked expletive. Enzo turned to see him plucking another hair-thin needle from the back of his husband's arm. Sander's face went dead white. "Not again, Tarik. I can't live through that again."

He supposed they were lucky. Most of the people in the box had powers like Jim's or Princess Katlin's, or the King Consort's. Even out of control, they didn't cause any physical harm. But Princess Odile and the Duke of Roses alone were enough to cause massive destruction.

The Royal Guard had all drawn their weapons, which did no good without a target. The immediate problem was the people they were here to protect. They could hardly shoot them.

Enzo stilled. *They* couldn't shoot the princess and the duke, but he could. Not shoot them, but incapacitate them and render their powers unusable, at least for a while.

He hesitated, thinking through the idea and looking for flaws.

Without warning, an ominous rattling began. A strange vibration accompanied the sound. Every table and chair the box shook in unison. Sander moaned and collapsed against Tarik. "I should never have stopped wearing the containment glove."

Magnetism. The table and chair legs were all metal and reacting to the Duke of Roses as his power began to leak out control. Two metal water pitchers flung itself through the air without warning straight at the king. Fortunately, Bastien's power reacted faster and they collided in mid-air before reaching him. The king's eyes widened as they crashed into one of his guards instead. Even the royal power was haywire if Bastien couldn't control how the deflection functioned.

Sander's face took on a look of intense concentration. Gradually the vibration from the tables and chairs subsided to an erratic rattle.

The wind picked up. Programs and small objects in the front half of the box were swept into the building cyclone.

He was out of time.

He turned toward Odile. He needed to see her for this to work. Pressure built in his chest.

Rrrrrrrbbbbbbbttttttt

The princess disappeared. The wind stopped abruptly.

For half a second, there was utter silence in the box, then everyone began yelling at once. A dozen weapons were pointed at him. Amid all the shouting, the vibration of metal legs rattling against the floor began to build again. The building shook with an ominous groan. In a flash of horror, Enzo realized the metal supports of the entire structure were reacting to the duke's magnetism.

He didn't have time to explain. He raised his hands and stepped back, away from the king and the other royals. One step, two. He could see everyone except Jim, who was still behind him.

A tiny prick stung his throat. He'd been hit, but it wouldn't matter. He only hoped the king's deflection power would recognize what he was about to attempt.

The pressure built.

Rrrrrrrrbbbbbbbttttttt

Bastien, the royals, the guards, and everyone else disappeared.

The screaming stopped. The tables and chairs hit the floor in a single, mighty crash. The groan of twisting metal stopped.

Everything was blessedly silent.

His power was building again, demanding release. The drug, he supposed.

Rrrrrrrrbbbbbbbttttttt

The force of the call shook him, but did no other damage.

Enzo looked around the room, the reality of what he had just done sinking in. Dozens of frogs hopped in every direction. Among them were the king of North Abarra, a prince, two princesses, two dukes, and a score of other royals. He did a frantic scan of the area, looking for exit points and hoping they would be safe enough as long as the doors were locked.

Rrrrrrrrbbbbbbbttttttt

He breathed through the aftermath and continued his assessment.

Without the two hulking guardsmen stationed in the rear, another row of seats was visible in the very back of the box. Enzo realized there was one person all of them had forgotten. Someone small, but not insignificant.

Lori Calhoun, aka The Wasp.

Lori smiled at him from the corner. She was wearing a pair of headphones. On the table next to her were a diet soda, her tablet, her phone, and what looked like a box of cigarettes.

He wasn't sure about The Wasp, but he had never seen Lori smoke.

His chest ached. He could feel the power just under his sternum, waiting to burst out like a bad case of the hiccups.

Rrrrrrrbbbbbbbttttttt

The reverberations left him gasping. Lori, safe in her headphones, remained stubbornly human.

Their eyes met, she winked, then jumped out of her chair and screamed, "Jim, he's out of control, stop him!"

Truth, Enzo realized. Nothing but the truth.

"Jim, he's out of control. Stop him!"

Lori's command brought home two points simultaneously, freezing Jim in place. Her words carried the essence of truth, and certainly the number of toads scattered across the floor proved her claim.

But Enzo had looked right at her and done his thing, and she was still on two legs. That alone gave Jim pause.

He stood some four feet behind Enzo, with a relatively clear, frog-free stretch of floor between them.

"Get him," Lori demanded. She reached behind her back and brought out one of her pet Glocks. "You take him down, or I will." She raised the pistol and damned if she didn't cock the thing. "Now."

If nothing else, Jim needed to get Enzo out of her way. He gathered himself and lunged, aiming to pull Enzo into the clear spot of floor. There were things the CIA could forgive, but squashing an Abarran royal when they were in toad form would not make the list.

Enzo went down easily, almost as if he wanted have someone else take control. Jim scrambled over him, pinning his shoulders and knees to the ground.

"What are you doing, Lori?" Jim craned his neck to see her. She still had the Glock pointed in their direction, grinning at him like this was all some kind of game.

Underneath Jim, Enzo grimaced and retched, his eyes pressed shut. His belly heaved against Jim, distracting him so he didn't notice Lori's approach until her pistol's muzzle brushed Jim's ear. He jerked away. "What the fuck are you doing?"

The gun moved and she laughed, twirling it on her fingertip. Why hadn't Lori turned into a toad like everyone else Enzo looked at? Jim had avoided being zapped because he'd been standing out of range behind Enzo. Lori had been right there. She should have gone amphibian with the rest of the crowd.

Except...those headphones. Maybe hearing the sound Enzo made played a part. Without giving himself time to think, Jim snatched the headphones off his sister, his eyes shut so he wouldn't accidentally cross gazes with Enzo.

With a **Rrrrbbbbtttt** as loud as a gong being struck, Enzo did his thing. By the time Jim opened his eyes, a small tree frog hopped onto the handle of his sister's Glock.

Jim lurched to his feet, heading for the nearest table. He grabbed a wineglass from one of the disordered place settings and, before Lori-the-frog could hop any further, he nudged her off the pistol and trapped her under the glass.

"Well." Jim sat back on his heels, staring down at his sister.

"Well." Enzo answered him. He was sitting up, legs bent, head between his knees.

"Too much yoga."

"What?"

"Only someone who does too much yoga could sit like that without busting a ball."

Enzo snorted and shook his head, surveying the scene. Toads of all different shapes and colors were scattered over the floor. Chairs lay overturned, centerpieces discarded. "Any guesses what happened?" he asked, his voice harsh in the sudden quiet.

Jim kept a hand on the glass covering his sister. "I have no fucking idea. You're the local. You tell me how supos work."

"Not like that."

The unexpected male voice from across the room made Jim jump. King Bastien squatted on the floor in the opposite corner. Despite his awkward position, his trousers still had their crease, and he was definitely human.

"You haven't zapped me like that since we were kids," Bastien said to Enzo.

"It wasn't intentional." Jim shifted closer to Enzo. "Something tried to influence all the supos in the crowd."

"Something or someone," Enzo said. "Shooting darts that must have carried some kind of drug. I felt it" — he kept his gaze on his hands — "like I'd been stung by a wasp or something."

"A wasp, or The Wasp." Bastien gave Jim a pointed look. "Where'd your sister go?"

Jim stared at the frog under glass, wondering what the hell she'd done.

CHAPTER NINETEEN

King Bastien convened a meeting in Princess Odile's office conference room, a space immediately adjacent to the desk Lori had used during her days as Lori Lapin.

Jim grimaced at the memory, one superseded by the much more recent impression of her pistol so close to his ear. Before leaving the royal box, he and Enzo had found a dozen or so inch-long darts, so slender they were almost like hypodermic needles without the attached syringe. Someone had shot them at the royals, and since shooting was his sister's favorite game, he had a disquieting suspicion that Lori had violated these people in a very basic way. The thought left him distraught.

Besides the king and Enzo, Princess Odile and her consort the Duke of Champagne had seats at the table, as did Nico, the king's husband. On the far end,

Teo had assumed control of the glass still encasing Lori, with Agent S and Agent M flanking him.

Because yes, the magnetic storm set off by the Duke of Roses had attracted more than their attention.

If he had to guess, Jim would have said the clock hadn't hit 2200 yet. Herve was unaccounted for, as was Armand, and Teo had delegated the clearing of the grounds to other members of the King's Guard. There were any number of supos who needed comforting — if someone as strong as Princess Odile looked wrecked, the others must be a mess — so Teo delegated that task, too.

Jim sat gingerly in the seat next to Enzo, who had the haunted look of someone living out their worst nightmare. Jim might get painted with the same dubious brush as his sister, but he couldn't make himself leave Enzo's side.

King Bastien knocked on the tabletop to gather everyone's attention. He was calm, composed, his royal party clothes as fresh as if they'd just come from the cleaners, and if all eyes were on him, his eyes were on Jim. "I understand that you and your sister are agents of the CIA but you're here in an unofficial capacity."

Jim straightened in response to the king's authoritative tone. Bastien clearly didn't have time for fools. *This oughta go well.* "As I've told Enzo and the representatives from the Ministry's Security Division—"

Jim was interrupted by a flurry of movement at the end of the table. Teo had been knocked aside, the wine glass crashing on the marble floor. One moment she'd been a toad, but now Lori was present in person.

"What'd I miss?" she asked, giving Jim a wink, disturbing in its normality. King Bastien's appraisal didn't seem to fluster Lori, and if she'd been upset by her sudden transformation, she didn't let it show.

She did toss an annoyed glare over her right shoulder where Teo stood glowering at attention. Agents S and M gave her more space, but still kept to their positions on either side of her. Something about Lori's jubilation in the royal box, along with the way she'd avoided Enzo's power with headphones, had Jim equally on guard. She was involved in something serious, and he had no idea if he could help her.

Or if he should.

"Your brother was just explaining why you're both here." King Bastien reestablished his control of the situation.

Lori crossed her hands on the table, her relaxed posture communicating confidence. "We missed our old family stomping grounds, so we came to check things out."

"Came to check things out?" the king echoed.

"Sure." She glanced at Jim. "We've heard about your all our lives and figured it'd be fun to see the royals in their natural habitat."

Jim blinked. "That's not quite true." He glanced at Enzo. "I tracked chatter on the dark web pointing at threats against Princess Odile. We wanted to see if we could help."

Lori smirked. "What he said. And since the princess's dear event planner got so sick, it was a good thing I showed up, right?" She looked around as if just realizing where she was. "What's going on in here? It feels like someone's on trial or something."

Enzo's expression went from distant to unreadable.

Bastien crossed his arms, gaze locked on Lori. "Someone appears to have drugged many of the royals in attendance tonight, causing them to lose control of their powers."

"That sucks." She looked concerned, but to Jim's eye, not concerned enough. He knew his sister better than anyone, and her flippant attitude covered anger and...fear?

Enzo shifted in his seat and again Jim tried to catch his glance. This time he was successful and they shared a wordless moment, one that left Jim even less certain. Then Enzo reached over and wrapped a hand around Jim's wrist. *Warmth. Strength. Comfort.* Jim slipped his hand around and interlaced their fingers.

Either he trusts me or he wants to have something to grab in case I try to run.

Someone knocked firmly on the conference room door. Before anyone could respond, the door swung open and Herve shoved Armand through. Armand's hands were bound behind his back and Herve carried a leather satchel.

"Pardon me, your highness" — Herve tipped his head at the King — "but I found this man attempting to leave the grounds in the middle of a crowd of guests. He carried this." Herve dropped the satchel on the table. "Which contained this."

He unzipped the satchel and pulled out a small handgun. "This little treasure is capable of shooting these." He lifted out a small packet containing thin silver darts, exactly like the ones Enzo and Jim had found in the royal box.

Jim's attention was drawn to Lori, who tensed when the darts were brought out. Her face had gone pale, and the realization that she was likely involved sat like a pool of acid in Jim's gut. He tightened his grip on Enzo's hand, taking cold comfort in the fact that Enzo didn't pull away.

"And I learned one other thing." Herve drew himself up to his full five feet, eight inches. "I learned who Royal Pain is."

He looked right at Lori when he spoke, his words landing like a blow. She sat very still, her spine straight, her lips pressed together.

"Royal Pain is the name of one of the radicals who was making threats against the princess," Enzo said to the King.

Bastien thanked him and turned his attention to Herve. "Are you going to keep us in suspense?"

"With the information from the American," Herve gestured to Jim, "I was able to confirm that the one called Royal Pain was here on the estate and was also involved in planning the event."

Twin spots of color started on Lori's cheeks, and if everyone was listening to Herve, they were all watching her.

"I also found evidence suggesting Royal Pain had links with the radical group formed by Umberto da Silva, a group that seems to have been involved with some kind of internal dispute that may have resulted in Mr. da Silva's death." He glared at Armand as he spoke. Armand responded with a scoffing sound.

Enzo drew his hand away from Jim. "This evening in the royal box, something affected my control, and strangely, Miss Calhoun was the only one who knew enough to wear headphones. I can't alter someone if they can't hear me."

"Your supo didn't bother Jim," Lori said, fingers intertwined so tightly her knuckles turned white.

"He was behind me, out of range. Besides, I've changed him more than once, so I know he's sensitive to my power."

"Be careful," Lori said softly. "It would suck if you lost control again."

"I lost control, too," Princess Odile said, her voice wavering. She cleared her throat and began again, sounding more like herself. "Someone did something to me. If not for Enzo, I could have blown everyone off the face of the earth."

She faced Lori, her question unstated. Bastien watched Lori too, tapping a kingly finger against his lips. "Why?" he finally asked.

Lori shook her head, her expression a mix of anger and relief. "We're Abarran, but we didn't grow up here, and I bet none of you give a shit."

Her only response was silence.

"Because you fools can't all get along. Dad was from North Abarra and Mom grew up in the South, and they had to immigrate to the States to be together." The anger in her tone grew with each word.

"Why did you kill Umberto?" Enzo asked quietly.

"She didn't." Armand glared at all of them. "He lost his nerve and threatened to give me up. Said the drug was too dangerous, as if you didn't deserve everything that happened and more."

A shocked silence greeted Armand's declaration, one broken by the king. "Get him out of here," he said, and Herve pulled Armand out of the room.

That left Lori on her own. Jim cleared his throat, his attention fully on the sister he loved. "You're Royal Pain."

Lori gave a quick look around, then raised her chin. "I demand to talk to my lawyer."

"Teo." Enzo gave one of his one-word lectures.

King Bastien stood, as did the princess and her consort. "Escort Miss Calhoun and her brother to Security and call their lawyer. The local police will need to be called, too."

Jim didn't move. He couldn't. "What have you done?" he whispered.

"Something you didn't have the balls to do." Lori laughed bitterly.

Agent M came around the table toward Jim, but Enzo stopped him. "Bastien, I'll vouch for Jim. I don't believe he had anything to do with this."

The king gave Enzo a long look, then nodded. "Just the sister, then."

Jim got up because he didn't know what else to do. He followed Enzo out of the conference room, out of the main house, and off the princess's property.

Only when they were safe in Enzo's cabin, with the door shut against the world, did he cover his face with this hands and let go.

Once again, the most dangerous man he knew was in his home and Enzo didn't know what to do with him. Bastien hadn't questioned his decision to offer asylum. Enzo hadn't stopped questioning it.

He supposed he should try and get Jim to talk. Theoretically, they had much in common: their jobs, being of Abarra but not strictly Abarran, super powers that were State secrets...close family relations with terrorist tendencies.

Enzo made tea and, for the time being, let his home be what Bastien had let him provide. A sanctuary.

For the first time since he had known him, Jim offered information up first.

"I should have known."

"Maybe." But Enzo hadn't known his father was involved with the same group. Was it more or less of an excuse that his father had been estranged? Enzo had never felt a close personal connection to Umberto. Lori had not only been Jim's sister, but his partner. The person he should have been able to trust above all others. Enzo couldn't fathom the betrayal.

As an agent of the crown, he supposed he should consider the idea that betrayal hadn't entered into the picture. He tried not to think about why he hadn't pursued that line of inquiry. Umberto he didn't trust. Lori he didn't trust. But Jim ...the man with the secrets...he had offered his home. Not because he thought he could breach his defenses, but because he thought the man needed the protection.

"This trip was her idea." Jim gave a short laugh. "That should have been my first clue. Our whole life she's wanted nothing to do with Abarra. Then suddenly, we have to save the princess. I thought she was finally ready to explore our roots. I thought the princess was just an excuse for her seek out some of our Abarran cousins."

"She never talked about Abarran politics?"

"Not even a little. I was the one who took all the history classes. My parents loved Abarra — not North, not South. Just Abarra — but the political situation was different then. I think there were things they never told us about our heritage. Why we had to change our names, for example."

"You both have powers," — Enzo held up a hand when Jim would have interrupted — "whether you accept them or not. Your parents most likely did, too. It would have complicated things if they wanted to leave the country permanently, especially a generation ago."

Enzo stared at his cup of untouched tea. "When I was little I used to listen to my mother talk about her homeland. She had so many good memories, I loved Abarra because she did. Then I got older, took the history classes, poli-sci...I'm American, when it comes down to it. I don't believe in power by birthright."

"Abarra is a constitutional monarchy. We have a parliament," Enzo pointed out. "And the king can't rule without sufficient powers. The powers make for a unique situation."

"Powers which are hereditary," Jim said, "and which each potential monarch is either born with or without. The powers don't make someone a good person or a wise ruler. You can't acquire powers through hard work, or intelligence, or public service. You might as well say the king must have green eyes."

Enzo wasn't sure he disagreed. "It's the right of Abarran citizens to choose whether to continue the monarchy. We elect a parliament and prime minister. If they wish to further restrict or challenge the powers of the monarchy, Abarrans must do so themselves."

"Well, maybe someone should consider it," Jim shot back. Then he slumped even lower. "Fuck. I was the one with the seditious rhetoric. I used to talk shit all the time, but it was freshman poli-sci posturing. It was never personal or actionable for me like it obviously is for Lori."

He gazed up at Enzo. "What if it was me? What if I was the one who planted the seed in her head to overthrow the monarchy?"

Enzo picked up Jim's cup and went back into the kitchen. He dumped the untouched tea into the sink. Then he fished around in the cabinets until he found Zha Zsi's emergency stash. Back in the living room, he splashed a healthy dose of patxaka into both their cups.

"Santé."

"You don't drink," Jim observed dully. But after a second, he picked up the cup and tossed it back. He grimaced and wiped a hand across his mouth. Patxaka obviously didn't rate the same adoration as Abarran wine. Or maybe it wasn't the drink. He looked defeated. "People are hurt and not just royals. It's my job to prevent shit like that."

Enzo drank his own shot, the tangy sweet flavor oddly grounding. He didn't point out that the CIA had a long history of shit exactly like that. "Did you introduce her to any of these terrorists?"

"What? No!"

Enzo refilled their cups. "Salud."

"Are you kidding? I couldn't even get you to have a second glass of wine."

"Party's over. I'm on my own time." Enzo didn't wait. The second cup slid down easier than the first. The faint aroma of licorice lingered between them as Jim followed suit.

Third cup. Enzo simply poured and waited.

"Is this an Abarran interrogation technique?" Jim asked before he tossed back the shot.

"Were the terrorists sanctioned by the CIA? Are you working for the South Abarran government?"

Jim refilled their cups. He raised his glass. "Fuck you."

"Cheers," Enzo corrected.

There wasn't enough liqueur in the bottle to get truly drunk. Enzo doubted double the amount would have loosened Jim's tongue any more than the shock of the day's events had done. In fact, by the time the last drop was gone, he had become less talkative. Some of the blankness had faded from his eyes, but it was replaced by wariness and something that, in another man, might have been regret.

Enzo stood and gestured toward the stairs.

"Let's get you to bed. There's going to be plenty to sort tomorrow." There would be plenty to sort for months, but tomorrow sounded more doable.

Jim followed him up the stairs and down the hall without comment.

Neither of them paused at the door to Enzo's room, although the temptation was an ache deep in his chest. Enzo opened the door to the guestroom and gestured inside. "The sheets should be clean. Check the closet, there are usually some abandoned clothes in there. You're welcome to anything you find."

The little speech sounded rough. The offer was genuine, not a lie. Still, he wondered if the spy would hear what he really wanted, the things he couldn't ask for.

Jim paused in the door, surveying the room.

He moved, and Enzo braced himself to turn away.

Jim's hand fisted in his shirt, his body hard against him as he pushed him inside and closed the door.

"We can't," Enzo got out. "You've been drinking and..." He trailed off, not sure how to express the obvious emotional trauma. "I don't want to take advantage of...."

Jim laughed, amused with a mean edge. "You're the lightweight when it comes to drinking. I'm fine." He moved forward again, still with the handful of shirt so Enzo was trapped close enough to smell the patxaka — anise and apples — on his breath. He pulled his arm in closer, so they were chest to chest, only the width of his fist apart.

He should move away, but Enzo felt his body swaying toward the other man.

Jim leaned closer, bending a little so their heads were side by side. Warm breath tickled Enzo's ear. "Tell me you don't want this, and we can stop."

Enzo froze, trying to find logic instead of emotion. "I don't think sex is a good idea after ...."

"Do you want it?"

They shouldn't. But should had nothing to do with want. For once in his life, his ability to control his desires for the greater good was irrelevant. He stared at the ceiling trying to label the strange, light feeling in his chest. Freedom, maybe.

"No."

"Liar." The word was soft, almost a sigh. There was nothing soft about the kiss. The hand not in his shirt cupped the back of Enzo's head — rough at first, as though he might try to escape — then, as the kiss deepened, as if he simply needed to keep him as close as possible.

Enzo closed his eyes and angled his head for better penetration.

Jim growled as he took advantage. His grip on Enzo's shirt finally loosened as his fingers went to work on the buttons.

Enzo's own hands pulled Jim's polo out from his waistband. The damn wire was finally gone. Thank god. He had intended to push the shirt up over Jim's head, but got distracted by hot, smooth skin. He opened Jim's pants instead and shoved his hands inside to cradle lean hips. He traced his thumbs over the curve of bone and ridges of muscle. He wanted to linger, to explore everything, but Jim had finished with the buttons. He grabbed the back of Enzo's shirt and pulled. Enzo's hands were yanked down with the fabric and trapped by his side, almost behind his back.

Jim growled approval. His lips moved to Enzo's neck, his shoulder, his pecs. He pushed Enzo backward until they were on the bed, Enzo's arms still trapped in the shirt, Jim pinning him to the bed.

"What do you want?"

The words were punctuated by sharp teeth on his nipple and Enzo understood that Jim wasn't looking for tenderness, or understanding, or care. He needed control and the temporary oblivion of the flesh.

"You," he gasped, knowing the one word held more truth than Jim might want to hear.

Whatever he heard, it seemed it was enough. Jim went to work feverishly removing clothes. His lips and teeth and hands seemed everywhere, until Enzo lost coherent thought.

"Lube?"

He scrambled for the drawer next to the bed, relieved to find condoms as well. Then Jim pushed him down, face into the pillows. Enzo raised his hips and pushed back against the tongue and fingers at his entrance, moaning and thrusting desperately. Jim moved again, one hand on Enzo's back, the head of his cock between Enzo's cheeks, just out of reach.

"Tell me again."

"Yes."

"Truth." Vicious. Possessive.

After all the urgency, he was careful as he pushed in. Careful and deliberate until Enzo surrendered and begged. Until Enzo had no thought of comfort, only need. Until both of them found oblivion.

CHAPTER TWENTY

He should go to his own room.

The room was still dark. His belly itched with his own dried seed matted in the hair on his abdomen.

One of them had pulled up the sheets.

He wondered if one of them had disposed of the condom or if it had been left where it fell. It felt as if this was a question that could wait for the morning.

Next to him, Jim had curled into a tight ball.

He should go to his own room. Jim might want his privacy in the morning.

Instead, he rolled to his side and curled around the other man.

When he woke again he was alone in the bed. The angle of light through the window indicated the day was still young.

Downstairs Zha Zsi had cleared away the empty patxaka bottle and was rinsing the cups in the kitchen sink.

He stood in the doorway watching her. There was no use asking her where she had been last night when he was making a fool of himself.

"Jim?"

"Gone," she said serenely, "and his boat. The girl we still have. The CIA wants her back. They haven't said what they will do with her."

"I see."

Enzo wondered if his own face had the same blank look Jim's had after his sister had been arrested. There were reports and meetings and a million details to take care of.

The kingdom must be in chaos. All royals were still under threat from the new weapon. He had most certainly blown his cover with the princess.

"The wine at the campsite has been sent to a lab. In addition to Armand, we have uncovered sympathizers in the Ministry of Powers." His mother was still talking, summarizing what the king's agents had been doing after he abandoned his post.

None of it seemed important. He felt disconnected, the kitchen where he had grown up looked foreign and oddly unreal — the light through the window too bright and the shadows in the corners too deep.

Perhaps this was the letting go Master Inigo always talked about, although he doubted he should feel so unmoored from reality.

His mother came and put her arms around him. Enzo realized he hadn't seen her in over eighteen months. She had grown her hair longer and it had more silver streaks. He rested his chin on her head and hugged her back until the world settled a little.

"How much trouble am I in?"

She shook her head. "Always the good boy. You worry about the wrong things, my son."

Enzo thought worrying he had let a potential terrorist escape the country might not be considered the wrong thing by most people, but Zha Zsi never thought like anyone else. Her own life was a tightwire act between causes she believed in and methods she couldn't condone.

"I let myself be ruled by my desires. I put myself before the safety of others. Master Inigo would be disappointed."

"Enzo," her voice was troubled and she drew back so she could look up at him. "Master Inigo's job was to teach a young boy to control his powers. He never meant for you to suppress your own needs or mistrust your instincts."

She let him go and stepped back. "You should check your email."

That, he supposed, was his cue to get to work. But when he opened his laptop, it wasn't encrypted messages from the Royal Guard he found.

He plucked the post-it off the screen. There was no message, no goodbye, just a name, Anthony Bennett, with an address and phone number.

CHAPTER TWENTY-ONE

Jim let the letter sit, unopened, for a good three days. The heavy cardstock and elegant script would have identified the sender, even if it hadn't been sealed with a dob of wax impressed with King Bastien's royal insignia. September in Napa was just too darned gorgeous to deal with anything unpleasant. While some of his memories — Enzo da Silva's dark eyes, for example — were exquisite, he wanted to leave behind much of what had happened in Abarra.

In the end, though, the guilt did him in. He'd promised his mother he'd take care of his sister. Knowing Lori was stuck in an Abarran jail prodded at him, making it harder and harder to ignore the royal missive.

Once the CIA got hold of Lori's escapade, they'd both been put on leave, and quite frankly, Jim didn't care if he ever went back. He sat on his back deck, an expanse of flagstone with territorial views of the surrounding hills. Wine country.

They made wine in Abarra, too, north and south.

Still sticky from the game of tennis he won, he picked at the letter's wax seal. As had become his habit, he squelched the little burst of hope that this would have anything to do with the most intriguing person in North Abarra. King Bastien had better things to do than play Cupid.

His neighbor and tennis partner had gone home for a quick shower but would be back for happy hour, a time limit that gave Jim the push he needed to open the letter. *Do it now before you talk yourself out of it.*

Mr. Jim Calhoun
Napa, California

Dear Mr. Calhoun,

On behalf of His Majesty, King Bastien of North Abarra, I wish to extend a formal invitation to return to our fair country. Given the results of the calibration you underwent with the Ministry of Powers, you would be an asset to our Intelligence Bureau and a position has been created with you in mind. His Majesty recognizes the loyalty you demonstrated during those difficult days last summer and would like to reward you for your efforts.

Please contact me with your response at your earliest convenience.

Sincerely,
Corin Vidal,
Secretary to His Majesty the King

"Well slap my ass and call me *Sorpresa*," he murmured. The letter included a postscript with the secretary's email address for the most efficient correspondence. Quickly, before he could lose his nerve, he grabbed his laptop.

I won't kill anybody for you.

Despite the time difference, Vidal's response was immediate.

You won't have to.

Jim paused, fingers on the keyboard. He believed in the power of threes, and if he counted the email as one factor and his responsibility toward Lori as a second factor, he just needed one more to seal the deal.

The doorbell rang and he peeled himself out of the wooden chair, annoyed with his neighbor for coming to the front door when he could have just walked around the house. "You knew where I'd be."

Yes, he was talking to himself, but living alone in a four-bedroom house with winery views from every window would do that to a person. He kicked off his shoes at the back door and padded across the hard wood floors, ready to give Neighbor Bob some grief.

Instead of his neighbor, he opened the door to find a delivery man who asked to see his ID, then handed over a large box.

Half a case of Royal Roses Red. The joint venture between wineries in North and South Abarra. Nicely symbolic, and sent anonymously. Or almost anonymously. Instead of a card, the sender had drawn a pair of frogs on the inside of the box's lid. The frogs were looking at each other and smiling.

The third factor fell into place.

October in Abarrra felt much like October in Napa, without the tourists. Jim guided his new Citroën over the winding road between Lesrochers and Princess Odile's estate. No one knew he was coming — that had been deliberate — and rather than dwell on his possible reception, he forced himself to stay in the moment. The car ran smoothly and almost too fast, the air was warm but not hot, and there was a gentle contrast between the gold-tinted fig tree leaves, evergreen pines, and the bracing blue of the ocean.

Rather than approach from the graceful main entrance, he turned into a narrow gravel road just past the driveway. He'd plotted his course by GoogleMaps because while he respected the princess and her consort, he didn't want to deal with any awkwardness.

Seeing Enzo for the first time in four months had enough potential for discomfort.

Maybe.

He hoped not.

The gravel road ran along the edge of the olive grove, then into a stand of cypress. This close to

Enzo's cabin, nerves twisted Jim's belly, a ticklish feeling that made him grimace. "He sent you a case of wine. That must mean something."

Jim just didn't know what.

Enzo's cabin looked much the same, except the grapevines covering one wall had turned orange, bronze, and scarlet. Jim parked the Citroën on the far side where it wouldn't be easily seen. He went around to the boot to retrieve the pair of large picnic baskets, though he left his overnight bag in the car.

Didn't want to be presumptuous.

Approaching the front door, he made a quick assessment of the scene. Things felt calm, quiet, but not deserted. Jim couldn't explain how he determined the difference, but he was confident he was right. Which meant Enzo must be somewhere on the princess's estate. "Maybe pruning elephants," Jim murmured.

He fully expected Enzo had armed his alarm system before leaving for the day. Squinting, Jim scanned the doorframe, looking for wires or sensors. Alerting Enzo to his presence wasn't the worst thing in the world. After all, Jim had come all the way from Lesrochers to see him. "All the way from Dulibre. Hell, all the way from Napa."

He shook his head. Enzo had sent him Abarran wine, as good as an invitation as far as Jim was concerned.

The door was locked, which delayed him a minute or so, and crossing the threshold set off a quick, high-pitched beep. Jim hoped Enzo wouldn't zap first. Or zap him before he could get any words out. "Still can't believe he turned me into a damned frog."

Chuckling, Jim went to work unpacking the baskets. The room was as he remembered: spare furnishings beautifully made, carefully selected art, and zero clutter. He'd brought a selection of Californian wines and a dozen or so small plates from a restaurant near his flat. He opened a bottle of red to breathe and set a bottle of pinot grigio in a bowl of ice. He'd turned his back to rifle through the kitchen cupboard, searching for wine glasses, when he heard a quick intake of breath.

"Surprise." Jim pivoted to stare down Enzo's blank expression. "I've brought dinner," he said, gesturing at the spread of food. "Would you prefer red or white?"

"What are you doing here?" Enzo spoke low, weighted down with surprise.

Jim shrugged, setting the wineglasses on the counter. "I wanted to see you." *I mean, you sent me wine, dude.* Jim glanced away long enough to grab the wine key and apply it to one of the bottles of white.

"I understand your sister is still in custody."

The reminder made Jim wince. "Yeah, the good ol' Abarran government has one-upped the CIA. She's here for trial and then for the length of her sentence." He didn't bother debating whether she'd be convicted. They had both witnessed her guilt.

"From what I understand, she might be able to save herself if she turns over the source of the drug."

Jim finished pouring the wine. "I can't speak to her loyalty, but we won't need her for that." He held out one of the glasses.

Enzo gave him a long look and accepted the wine. "We?"

Raising his glass, Jim gave him a soft smile. "We, as in me and my new partner at the North Abarran Intelligence Bureau. We've shut down the lab where the drug was made, and we're very close to cleaning up the leftovers." Their glasses clicked together. "Since my employers were kind enough to agree to my request to work from Lesrochers, here I am."

His expression went from reserved to confused. "Work from Lesrochers?"

"Dulibre's too far."

"From?"

Jim shrugged, feeling foolish. He'd prepared himself for being zapped on sight and tried to keep himself from anticipating a warm welcome of the physical kind. Blank confusion hadn't been on his list of things to worry about. "From you, Enzo da Silva." He gestured toward Enzo with his wineglass. "Take a sip. It's from my old neighbor's winery."

Turning the glass in his hands, Enzo stared into its depths. He took a sip, swirling the wine on his tongue. "It's good."

"They don't ship much outside the US, but there's a shop in Paris that sometimes carries the label."

Enzo's brows grew closer together. "Paris? You're serious."

"Yup. You're stuck with me for the foreseeable future." Jim chuckled and set his glass on the table. "And it's Etienne. Here in Abarra, I'm called Etienne." It had been an easy decision, really. Jim was part of his old life, and Etienne was his new.

All he sensed from Enzo was sincere confusion. He moved toward the landscaper-cum-Guardsman, going slow, giving him time to react. Enzo held his ground, so Etienne came closer. He took hold of Enzo's glass and set it behind him on the table, then took Enzo's hands in his own. "As much as I love my parent's homeland, you were by far the biggest incentive."

"We barely know each other."

"That's just it," Etienne said, pulling Enzo closer still. "We barely know each other, but what I know of you, I like."

"I don't believe you moved halfway around the world because of our little liaison... Etienne."

With a sigh, Etienne wrapped his arms around Enzo's waist. Enzo fisted his hands in Etienne's jersey, tight enough Etienne would have had to work to get away.

"King Bastien's offer was well-timed. I will admit that my sister's predicament influenced my thinking, but if I were just here for her, I would have stayed in Dulibre." He tugged again, closing the last inch so they were standing belly-to-belly. "And since she won't see me, I might as well have stayed in California. Now come on. Let's eat."

Enzo didn't move. "What if I said I was involved with someone."

That made Etienne laugh. If Enzo was seeing someone, he'd left no evidence of it anywhere. "I'm willing to take that chance. It's your secrets that intrigue me, after all, and I'm a very patient man."

Enzo's expression softened, not quite a smile but close. "And I am very stubborn."

Truth. Etienne closed the distance between them, pressing his lips to Enzo's in a gentle kiss. "You know what happens when an unstoppable force meets an immovable object, don't you?" he murmured against Enzo's lips.

"What?"

"Let's find out."

The End

Dear Reader,

Thank you for coming along on our adventure to Abarra!

We hope you enjoyed The Frogman and the Spy. This book is both completely different from anything we've written before and very much Liv & Irene.

*If you would like to explore some of our other work, you might enjoy **Vespers**, the book that launched our co-writing partnership. We think you'll find we've always enjoyed blending action and humor in paranormal worlds.*

You can see all our books, individual and co-written on Amazon. Many are also on Barnes and Noble, Kobo, Apple, and other major retailers.

*If you'd like to receive updates about new releases, sales, and giveaways, we invite you to join our Facebook group, **After Hours,** or sign up for our rather sporadic newsletter.*

We always love to hear from fellow readers, so come on by and say hello.

All the Best,
~Liv & Irene

ACKNOWLEDGEMENTS

A huge thank you to Chris Cox for inviting us to the Royal Powers universe. We both needed a break from the ordinary (do we *do* ordinary?) and this was definitely it. Thanks to EJ Russell for beta-reading and the family tree. Huge thanks to all the Royal Powers authors for loaning us your characters and world-building and answering all our questions.

Special thanks to Meg DesCamp for doing a phenomenal final edit round. (Meg's superpower is obviously speed-editing.)

Irene would like to thank Liv for sticking with the project after being turned into a frog by proxy (twice) and Bones and Kiddo, for telling her that, yes, turning people into frogs was hi-LAR-ious.

*Big shout-out to our **After Hours** crew who are always there to encourage us and make us smile.*

*Thank you. Thank you. Thank **YOU** for reading. We know you have many reading options and are always grateful and humbled when you choose us.*

Ps...Liv here....sending thanks to D. Ann Williams for a solid developmental edit that helped us focus the story, and to Fern Lee, our cover artist, for turning James Bond into a frog. (lol!) Also sending a huge thank you to my husband, for putting up with this writing thing.

Every project is different, and with each one Irene and I end up learning more about each other, and more about ourselves. This time we learned how to play, which is pretty cool. Thanks, partner!...and thanks so much to all of you for reading along!!

EXPLORE MORE
ROYAL POWERS

Want to meet the authors and get the latest
Royal Powers news?
Join the
Royal Powers Facebook Group!

Books about characters who appeared in
The Frogman and the Spy

Duking it Out by E.J. Russell
Sander, Duke of Roses and Tarik, Duke of Arles

King's Ex by E.J. Russell
King Bastien and Nico

The Marquis of Hidden Doors by Lynn
Lorenz
Remy Marchand

Pauper Prince Saves the Posh Pullet by
Chris Cox
The Honorable Mickey Zirubri

Royal Powers I

Duking It Out
by EJ Russell

The Hero and the Hidden Royal
by Renae Kaye

Marquis of Secret Doors
by Lynn Lorenz

The Lost Prince
by Sara York

Pauper Prince Saves the Posh Pullet
by Chris Cox

The Duke of Hand to Heart
by Jackie North

The Prince and the Pencil Pusher
by Kenzie Blades

A Merry Marquis Christmas
by Lynn Lorenz

Duke the Hall
by E.J. Russell

Our Gay Au Pair, Ell
by Chris Cox

Royal Powers II

King's Ex
by E.J. Russell

The Frogman and the Spy
By Irene Preston and Liv Rancourt

The Royal Gardener vs The Commoner Foreman
by Lynn Lorenz

and more to come….

ABOUT THE
AUTHOR

Say hello to the writing team of Liv Rancourt and Irene Preston. One day, Liv and Irene got the bright idea to play a game. Let's write a story about a vampire! We'll take turns! It will be fun!

In fact, they had so much fun they turned it into the **Hours of the Night** series.

And that was so much fun that they spun off another series called **Haunts & Hoaxes**.

And that was so much fun... well, you get the idea. So hang out, because you never know what we'll come up with next.

Irene
Irene Preston has to write romances, after all she is living one. As a starving college student, she met her dream man who whisked her away on a romantic honeymoon across Europe. Today they live in the beautiful hill country outside of Austin, Texas where Dream Man is still

working hard to make sure she never has to take off her rose-colored glasses.

Liv

Liv is a huge fan of paranormal romance and urban fantasy and loves history just as much, so her stories often feature vampires or magic or they're set in the past...or all of the above. When Liv isn't writing she takes care of tiny premature babies or teenagers, depending on whether she's at work or at home. Her husband is a soul of patience, her kids are her pride and joy, and her dogs – Trash Panda and The Boy Genius – are endlessly entertaining.

Thanks for reading along!!